I Used to Wear My Hair in Pigtails

Collected Poems and Stories of
EMILY MARJORIE CELLA

THE VAN DOREN COMPANY
Charlottesville, Virginia

I USED TO WEAR MY HAIR IN PIGTAILS.
COLLECTED POEMS AND STORIES OF EMILY MARJORIE CELLA

Copyright © 2005 by Joseph and Teresa Cella

Published by THE VAN DOREN COMPANY, 4852 Watts Passage, Charlottesville, VA 22911. 434-973-2201; fax 434-973-8964; e-mail vandorencompany@earthlink.net.

All Rights Reserved. No part of this publication may be reproduced or transmitted in any form or by any means, without permission in writing from the publisher.

ISBN 0-9679179-7-2

Printed in Canada

Publisher's Cataloging-In-Publication Data
(Prepared by The Donohue Group, Inc.)

Cella, Emily Marjorie.
  I used to wear my hair in pigtails : collected poems and stories of Emily Marjorie Cella.

  p. : ill. ; cm.
  ISBN: 0-9679179-7-2

1. Poetry, American--21st century. 2. Poetry--Women authors--21st century. 3. Short stories, American--21st century. 4. Short stories--Women authors--21st century. 5. Coming of age--Fiction. 6. Coming of age--Poetry. I. Title.

PS3553 .E555 2005
818.6/09   2005925109

Library of Congress Control Number: 2005925109

We owe a special debt of gratitude to Bill Van Doren and Laura Sutherland, the publishers, for their hard work, enthusiasm for the project and for truly understanding what Emily's book is really about.
  We are also deeply grateful to the many exceptional people who shared Emily's life.

— Joe and Terri Cella

Remembering Emily

Emily was born on August 31, 1983, the youngest of our four children. She was exceptionally close to her sister, Daina, and brothers Jay and Steve. The poems and short stories in this volume were composed between the ages of thirteen and nineteen.

She was wise beyond her years and bright with more humor than most comedians. She was kinder than the sweetest child; her faith, tolerance and loyalty were deeper than anyone could imagine. Her circle of friends encompassed the broad spectrum of her interests. She was, from the time she could write, a writer. She loved to write more than anything. She would write in notebooks at school while there was a lull between lessons. She wrote on pieces of paper that were lying around her room; she wrote on napkins if she was out and had no paper. She wrote little snippets in her address book, if that was all the paper she had. She was always thinking, always composing in her head. Her internet name was WhiMsiKal — she was certainly that. She always had a project, a subject, a theme she was writing and discussing. She was more interesting than any good novel. She had a way of reaching out and inviting you to dance the dance of life with her. Within her heart there was a strength and courage and a wondrous beauty. She was interested in everything.

She was an honor student in high school; she was a rising junior at Mary Washington College. She was the light in all of our lives. Three weeks shy of her 20th birthday, our daughter Emily Marjorie Cella was killed in a tragic automobile accident on August 7, 2003.

Contents

INTRODUCTION 1
ME 2
I USED TO 5
POTENTIAL 6
THE SPIRAL OF SUMMER 7
THE STARS ARE OUT 8
TWISTED 9
WARMTH 10
THE WORLD WORKS 11
TOPSY TURVY 12
WHAT ONE CAN KNOW 13
LOVE SUCKS 14
INTERNAL 15
WORDS 16
WHERE DO YOU SEE MY FACE? 17
THE LICORICE KIDS 19
TO FALTER 20
STARING 21
SPLIT SECONDS 22
SOMETIMES 23
SO I WAS YOUR SAVIOR 24
WHAT IF 25
SHE SITS ALONE 26
YOU LOVE THE COLOR PURPLE 27
MIRROR 28
SHE GAZES 29
SAND CONSUMING 30
FELINE 31
RAINSTORM 32
PREDATOR 34
PORCELAIN 35

POISON	36
POE WRITING	37
PERSONAL RHYTHM	44
OPEN WINDOWS	48
NIGHT SWIMMING	49
EVE	50
MULTIPLE	51
MISTAKE	52
JOURNEY	53
LONELY	54
INDECISION	56
HEAVEN	57
WALKED THIS PATH	58
HUMAN BEINGS	59
LOOK INSIDE MYSELF	61
MY IDEALS	62
BLONDE	63
CHICKEN SUB	64
I LOOKED AT YOU	65
I GREW IN A TIME	66
I	67
ADOLESCENCE	68
A WITHERING ROSE	69
HE CAN'T BE ALONE	70
HE BREATHES	71
HAYWIRE	72
HAVE YOU WONDERED	73
TONES	74
FELINE PART II	75
SHADES OF PURPLE	76
ENTRAPMENT	77
EMOTIONALLY ANOREXIC	78

DENIAL	79
CONSUME	80
CONFUSION IS A RAINSTORM	81
CLOSURE	82
CHRIST	84
CHOCOLATE APHRODISIAC POISON	85
CATHOLICISM	86
FAITH	87
CANDLES	88
BLUE LIPS	89
BLACK PEARL	90
BENEATH THE DOWN	91
AURORA	92
SIT BY THE WINDOW	94
AS I LOOK AROUND	96
BUILT BY NATURE	97
WE LIVE NOT FOR OURSELVES	98
BLISS	99
BRUSHSTROKES	100

Friend Poems

STOP UNTIL THE EVENING STARTS	102
SUMMERTIME OF INNOCENCE	103
12 CIGARETTES TO FREEDOM	104
UNREACHABLE	107
WE	108
WE HAD EIGHT EYES	109
WE TRADED CHILDHOODS	110
YOU GLANCED AT ME	111
WHEN I RECALL A TRAMPOLINE	112
WE WERE YOUNG ONCE	113
THE LIGHT BEAMS	114

TALULA	115
SISTER	116
ON THE SHELF	117
ROBOTS	118
MAYBE	119
MAGNETIC	120
PICNIC	121
LET ME GO	122
JUST LIE NEXT TO ME	124
IS IT THE WAY?	125
I COULD PAINT THIS ON GLASS	126
HEATHER SAYS	128
HE LISTENS	129
HE	130
GLASS PRISONER	131
GIRL	132
FRIENDSHIPS	133
SPLINT	134
DAY DREAMING	135
AN ODE TO HIM	136
ABSTRACTED THOUGHTS	137
AN ODE TO A NAMELESS SOMEONE	138
ALICE	140
INCOHERENCE	142

Family Poems

MARJORIE	144
PROTECTOR	146
TO DAINA	147
TERESA'S SICKNESS	148
PEOPLE TELL ME	149
DAINA	150

TERRI	151
AS I READ	156
VOLCANO GIRL	158

Short Stories

WITH A LITTLE GUIDING LIGHT	160
WHEN YOU FINALLY UNDERSTAND	162
EXPRESSIONS	167
WHEN STATUES CRY	169
UNSPOKEN ACTIONS	173
WINTER OF THE SPRING	178
THE FIRST DAY	181
BARBIE STORY	183
GENESIS RELIVED	190
LOG #4	195
HOCKEY STICKS AND CIGARETTES	197
XYLOPHONE	204
LOG #5	207
RANT	209
RANT #2	210
SHE WAS THERE	211
SATURDAY NIGHT	212
TIME STORY	215
THE MUERTE	217
DIARY OF SOMEONE IN 1962	221
CONCLUSION	227

Introduction

When I look inside myself
I first see the fuzzy blackness of my insides
But I'm pushing deeper
Farther
Into the Hidden caves within my soul
Down There
There is a person that I need to get to know
And she smiles warmly
At the realization of my arrival
She asks if I will sit
And talk with her for awhile
So I make myself all cozy
Lying deep within my soul
And the words
That she shared with me
Are some I thought you'd like to know . . .

Me

I have blonde hair
I like the snow
I like the color of summer
I have my father's face
My mother's coloring
My own soul
I like to read
I've lived in four states
I used to wear my hair in pigtails
I've lied to friends
I like the taste of champagne
But my hair is still blonde
And I still have my father's face
But I probably won't always like
The taste of champagne
Or the color of summer
But maybe I'll start
Wearing my hair in pigtails again
I believe I can do anything
I write down everything I feel
Everything I know and experience
I listen to any music with meaning
I like art but cannot draw
I envy those who can
My life is a roller coaster of ups and downs
I cannot control
But my hair is still blonde
And I still have my father's face

And my mother's coloring
But I won't always like art
Or write everything I feel
But maybe I'll get control
I have a beautiful sister
A humorous brother
And a brother I absolutely adore
But I never see
I have siblings yet
Feel like an only child at times
I love my parents and they love me
Yet I don't understand them sometimes
I don't even understand myself
I laugh with friends
I cry alone
All for no reason at all
But my hair is still blonde
And I still have my father's face
My mother's coloring
And my own soul.

I Used To

I used to wear
My hair in pigtails
And believe in magic
I used to think
Friends could never hurt you.

Bad things only happened
To bad people
No one died
And love was so easy

My biggest fear
Was the monster in my closet
Or the demons of the shadows
My biggest problem
Was what to wear to school

Innocence is broken
Faith is lost
I grew up

Bad things happen all the time
People I love have died
And some of my friends have
Bruised my soul

But maybe I'll wear my hair
In pigtails again.

Potential

She has so much potential
    She has a light
Don't they see
    I am dying inside
Reaching for a hand
    To lift me up
I miss and fall
    Plunging to other depths
Cold rips through me
    Numbing my skin
My protection no longer felt
    My insides catch frostbite
They turn black and blue
    Then break off
Inside is nothing
    I am a hollow tree
That didn't make it through the winter
    As spring approaches,
I see my family grow,
    Spreading their green fingers to the sky
While I remain
    Brown and withered
And my life is cut
    By a METAL BEAST
As I fall ashamed to the ground
    I once stood so high above

The Spiral of Summer

I always knew it was going to end
I never fully attached myself
Always left a synapse so as not to get so close
I knew you would stray and I wasn't going to be
    a part of that pain
Your hurtful melody, quixotic rhythm
A line I say so many times it becomes cliche
But I still smell you
You live inside me and permeate my
    bloodstream with sharp reminders
How can you understand I never loved you
When I led such a theatrical performance
Come to think of it, I even had myself fooled

The Stars Are Out

The stars are out
The night is clear
I've got to get away from here
Trapped for too long
I see where I should go, I grab my shoes
And drop them down
I feel like walking barefoot.
Walking?
I feel like dancing
In the streetlights
Late at night
Pretending to be
Someone I'm not
Pretending to be beautiful
And I dance
Under streetlights
And a clear sky
And you wonder
Who I am.

Twisted

They all said I was twisted
Those damn conformists
Because I mixed their
Heaven and hell
And found the devil in God
Prophetic heretics
I was only thinking
I was only thinking
I was only thinking
But now you're all angry
Because I am believing.

Warmth

There is this warmth between
my front door and the glass door
that substitutes for a screen.
The inside of the house is chilly
the outside is cold
But in those two inches of space
there is a warmth I cannot describe.
It's almost tangible.
It fills me with a depth unknown
and I can't seem to sneak away
from it, as I try to fit my body
in a two inch layer of comfort.

The World Works

The world works
In mysterious ways
Who knows where we'll be
In the next few days

Bare feet
In the sand
Hand and hand
We stand
Reluctantly
Sadly
We let go
And I put my shoes on

Topsy Turvy

Onto your inside and into your desires
Never meant to burn your sexuality
Extinguished by our jealousy
God told me not to do that
But the pewter screams
From your finger cuts
Milking my sorrow evil
Open flesh that calls our blood
He reached inside me more than once
The minute I admitted pleasure

I respected you more than you'll ever fathom,
In your realm of self-indulgence.

What One Can Know

What one can know is
    Infinite
Unless plateau
    At the limit
Where they can no longer
    Define anything
Symbols
    (Vibrant emphasizers)
Lose recognition
And their distorted
    Version of Christ
        Becomes clear
To only one
For we are all infallible
    Follies of this thing
We call humanity
    And to say you've
Pushed your limit
    Is redundant

Love Sucks

It was 12:59
I wanted to write so bad
But I had no light
Because I didn't pay
My electric bill
I used the money to get a roll of film
Developed
Because there was a
Picture of you in it
I used the money to buy you a CD
Because I knew you
Would love it
I used the money
To pay your rent
So I would be close to you
It was 12:59
I wanted to write so bad
I had just come
From your abandoned apartment
To find an empty CD case
And I can't even
Look at your picture
Right now
Because I didn't pay
My electric bill.

Internal

You slurred your words
Like some sort of intoxicated monster
But I only smelt fear
In your breath
Whisper   laughter   shouting
I was incoherent at the time
Now abrupt and powerful
Pocketing my weaknesses like old dollar bills

I can climb without intimidation
Up and even down if I desire
Moving with a rhythm all my own
That you never could, or will, decipher
Wounded souls wear sunken brows
Upon small foreheads that bore nothing
Independence will cower at what I have found,
For I have found indifference.

Words

Their words sank deep

Abandoning all principles
                They circled around her
"Wolves,"
                She thought
        Quivering she was their prey
        Empty bellies grumbling
        In the dead of winter
Cannibalistic instincts
        Overcoming all rational
Their words sank deep
        Like fangs
"Weakness!" they cried
Her eyes shed communal wine
                As they tore her away

Leaving naked marrow
To exist
        In a state
                Of self hatred

Where Do You See My Face?

Where do you see my face
Among the hollow streets
You walk your boulevard
To outrun my lie
And no one seems to seep
From veins
That have no heat
Love
You
Don't cry
See my heart beating
Underneath my skin
Walk forth from my footprints
Seated to the toes
Like you
Who fears to scream
Loud as I am

The Licorice Kids

Isn't it sad
The licorice kids
All peel themselves away
Peel themselves away
Finding nothing at the center
Empty candy wrappers
Trampled by careless feet
They are their own undoing
Own unwinding
As they peel themselves away
Shocked at every layer
Like little children
In the middle of the night,
It isn't right
To speak of such things
Dirty things
That those licorice kids know
As they peel themselves away
Peel themselves away
Leaving nothing sweet
To taste

To Falter

Before I trip
Into your vast decorum
Kiss me slightly
To give that longing feeling
Array of dirtiness
That struggles to shine
Like fluid movements
Past the skin
You wish you possessed
Half the craziness
You resent
Is love really restricted
      To the boundaries of your mind?

Staring

Staring out the window
Into a world that is so cruel
I saw a Benz drive by
And the driver had no shoes
Woman with a gold watch
Just strolled out of the welfare office
With the child she can't afford
And I start thinking about the
Impressions we receive or send
We worry so much about them
But God don't give a damn
He's the only one who knows
Where we're gonna end
She puts on an expensive dress
He scrapes the food left in the sink
He makes his living door to door
But who really gets less
And who is the one getting more
He rides his new bike
Adidas covers his feet
She watches him while
She sews the hole that ripped last week
He washes his new car
His neighbors look with despise
He neglects the little girl
With dirty hands and pleading eyes
And I start thinking about the impressions
We receive or send
We worry so much about them
But God don't give a damn.

Split Seconds

They see each other
Across the hall
For a second in time
They connect
And they see their life together
Would be lovers
Would be lives
If they could only reach
Each other's arms
He takes a step
She starts to turn
And then
The bell rings
And a beautiful life
Is thrown away
For the sake of not being late
To class

Sometimes

Sometimes I can almost
See a place behind the moon
Where everyone's dreams lie
The sky marks the brain
With synopses and Electro
Magnetic spectrums and
I fail to see the beauty

        I think you're brilliant
        But I've lost my magic pen
        So I can't tell you
        How enthralled I am with you
        Sinking slowly starts to stop

                I can't think today
                I watch her supervise
                And favorize
                And demoralize my self-esteem
                Sit back down
                At your clicking keys

So I Was Your Savior

So i was your savior
And bled secretly for you and all your failed
    excursions
When you were green and pretty
But now you lay with hands folded
In prayer choking that dove
As i struggle to breathe
And all i want to do is tell you i am sorry
For those sins
and i can't swallow down your faith and ideals
While i chase that poison with my own
    distorted reality
In which i've lived from youth
But only know, grown, you have a problem
    with.

Menstruation said to make me crazy
They won't trust anything that lives and bleeds
But doesn't really breathe
Talks of faded dreams and broken aspirations
To heal paper cuts
That melt and return like days
Slip away time until i am bleeding and
    refraining from breathing
As you're talking
Someone says "the kingdom of God is inside
    you"
Unless you're a woman.

What If

So what if I'm not something
At least I'm nothing
And nothing
Has no expectations to live up to
And nothing
Can do anything it wants
Because no one is bothered
By nothing
And if you were something fishing for
    compliments
With your light of a smile
And talent
Then you could be brought down
By everything
But I would be nothing
And my existence would be calm
And at least that's something
To look forward to.

She Sits Alone

She sits alone
On cement steps
Every day when I pass by
Her hands are
Twisted with arthritis
And every wrinkle is folded
Deep within the skin
For the years had
Walked upon her
Much too harshly
In her lifetime
A piece of broken heart
Twinkles in her eye
Long ago dulled
By the wariness of life
She wears a tattered sweater
Though it is eighty degrees
For it is her only piece
Of clothing besides
The ripped and battered pants
That don't match
In her pocket
She carries a picture
Of a beauty with long
Blonde hair
And eyes that glowed
Within their sockets
Her only possession
Is herself.

You Love the Color Purple

You love the color purple
Because it's one of those colors
That has so many different shades
Each one unique in itself
While still belonging to the others
All deep and rich
Poetry without words

You love the color silver
Because it's one of those colors
That can reflect all the others
And hide behind its shiny surface
Protected and secure
Song without music.

Mirror

She looked into the mirror
And didn't recognize the reflection
Her soul was gone
Skin giving no protection
Pieces of her
Slipping slowly away
But now it's all over
She died today
No matter how much she struggles
Or how much fights
Her emotions are flat
And she has lost sight
Pale face, expressionless eyes
Framed by blonde hair
And a mouth of lies
Her own teeth ate
Her soul away
She died today.

She Gazes

She gazes
As she wonders
Past the blankness
Deep into the lack of you
Distracted eating patterns
Mark your sorry path
On her
Breaking her slowly
Piece by piece
Too hateful not to let her
Shatter all at once
You give the illusion
Of love
The reality is you have
Nothing better to do
With your pathetic existence

Sand Consuming

Like Dry Sand
You filtered through my fingers
Leaving only grain
Inadequate and unfulfilling
For me to grasp
Thought the distance would heal
These burning wounds
But your absence was like oxygen
The back draft killed any hope
For another to love me
The way I let you love me
When I was willing and sane.

This man consumes
By her glass secret
What they're going to do
With skin like bruises
Or wild sound
Dark like your summers here
Me lacing your slender form
You say why we leave full
As I ask why I am empty

Feline

He waits to pounce
In the back of my reality
Like an afflicted feline
Salivating for revenge
Distracted eyes now focus in

    Fair and dry
    Stained with auburn

Adverse to his motives
In him I do not approve
I will never cede to him

Rainstorm

The rain slowly came like an air raid
    Rapidly increasing
It fell first upon my head
And seemed to seep through me
Creating a river
Of everything I wanted to extricate
Magnanimous claps of thunder
Snapped me back to my distorted reality
    That all I wished to cleanse was nothing that could
    Ever wash away with water
And even though I was set back,
To see the puddle below my feet was clear
    (and reflecting only film)
I tipped my head back and laughed with the lightning
for there is nothing better
Than becoming part of a rainstorm

Predator

He waits to pounce behind my mind
Salivating for his prey
What he wants he seeks to find
And he will get his blood today

    What I have done I do not know
    To come to greet this gruesome fate
    But now my limbs are bare, exposed
    My innocence succumbed to this

        But plants can't live without the rain
        And fruit will die without the sun
        So why do I, so frail remain?
        When so much was killed off so young

Porcelain

Though people are around
She is alone in herself
A porcelain Doll
Dressed up, face painted
Covered with frills and lace
To mask her otherwise hollow existence
Expressionless black beads
Cover the energy that is her mind
A natural actress has not blown her cover
Except to the one who admired her most
Her cheeks stained Red
In a permanent blush
That shows her insecurity

Poison

This turmoil so sudden
Swirled my stomach like paint
And made the color of you
Hunter green
Perhaps this blue
Years before your face will melt
Memory always served me well
Or pain
Whichever came first
In this look, this desire
Flux flux
Plucks dreams from the womb
That i poisoned
With this medication

Poe Writing

Once upon a midnight dreary, while I was
　　flying, bored and weary,
Over many a forest and wind with a cold and
　　biting roar,
When I ran into a house's siding, for my sight a
　　tree was blocking,
And so I got up and began knocking, knocking
　　on the front door.
"Open up already!" I muttered, but no answer at
　　the door —
　　　　　　　I did not feel like flying anymore!

Oh, distinctly I remember it was in that cold
　　December,
So cold I thought my beak would dismember,
　　and fall abruptly to the floor
Eagerly I wished to be inside — Hypothermia
　　was not the way I wished to die
So I fought to try, try to get into where it was
　　warm —
Oh how I wished to get inside where it was
　　warm —
　　　　　　　But it stayed closed, this door.

And so I stood uncertain, annoyed with the
　　burden
Angered me — filled me with madness never
　　felt before;

But, hark now, to still the anticipation of my
   soul, I stood station,
"'Tis some visitor entreating entrance at my
   chamber door —
Some late visitor entreating entrance at my
   chamber door —"
            This I heard and nothing more.

Presently my wings grew tighter, my patience —
   one inch wide, no wider
"Sir," said I, "or Madam, truly your forgiveness I
   implore;
But the fact is I was deprived, of the comfort
   you have inside,
And so I took a chance and arrived, arrived at
   your front door,
And maybe you could let me," — here he
   opened wide the door —
   And the idiot did not see me standing on the
                                         floor.

Deep into that dark ravine, long there he stood
   with me not seen,
Probably thinking stupid thoughts every human
   I'd encountered had thought before
But the silence was unbroken, and the stillness
   gave no token,
And the only word there spoken was the
   whispered word, "Lenore!"
This I thought was quite peculiar, so I repeated,
   "Lenore?"
            Merely this and nothing more.

And with that he went inside, leaving me
outside to die!
So I flew around the house even angrier than
before.
"Surely," said I, "surely he will hear me pecking
on his window pane"
And I found this human being to be even
dumber than before —
Yes, he stood there like a deer in headlights,
looking dumber than before
> He said, "'Tis the rain and
> nothing more."

"The rain?!" I thought he must certainly be
retarded, but then the window he slowly
started
To open and make for me a suitable door
Not any introduction made I; not a minute
stopped or stayed I;
But, after careful surveillance of the room I
perched on the ledge above his door
Perched upon a can of soda on the ledge just
above his door
> I'm sure that soda had been there a month
> or more.

Then after quite some while, this stupid twit
began to smile,
Like there was food stuck in my beak from
dinner the night before.
"Um, hi there bird from outside, must be too
cold to fly tonight,"

"DUH" I thought from inside, and my name he
did ask me for.
Why I do not know, but my name he did ask
me for.
                Quoth I, the Raven, "Nevermore."

Much he did ponder at what he heard so
plainly,
And no, my name was not what I had just said
before
But I could not stop myself from teasing, this
lowly human being
Staring dumbly at me from his place below me
on the floor,
Hair a mess, his face quite homely, looking up
at me from the floor
                He actually thought my name
                      was "Nevermore."

But I continued sitting warmly, though I know
this man would bore me
For I did not want to fly that night anymore.
And he started to utter, after I had not shaken
or fluttered
So he scarcely began to mutter, "other friends
have flown before —
On the morrow he will leave me, as my hopes
have flown before."
                Cruelly smiling I said, "Nevermore."

Startled by my reply, he let out an uneasy sigh
"Doubtless," said he, "what it utters is its only
stock and store,"

But I knew that he was undoubtedly frightened
It takes little to fool with a human such as him upon the floor,
Yes, naïve beings such as this one, scared standing on the floor
      By me the Raven and by "Nevermore."
At this I sensed him getting ticked, and this, in my sense of humor fit
To see his face get red and dance around like an idiot on the floor
"Please bird if you would be so kind, I see you there staring, I am not blind
I see you staring at me and I do mind, I mind you sitting above my door.
Would you please leave, or at least get the heck off my door?"
      Quoth I, the Raven, "Nevermore."

Then even I felt his temperature rise, and saw the angry sheen in his eyes
As he leaped at me, in vain, from his chair on the floor
"Wretch," he cried, "God has . . ." blah blah blah, I did not listen
For all he did was whine about some chick named Lenore
Heh, this girl must have dumped him, the chick named Lenore
      Quoth I (for fun), "Nevermore."

"Prophet!" said he, and he began yelling, knuckles white and face swelling,
Something about God and angels, and how he missed Lenore

Man it was sad, she had really gotten to him bad
To have him yelling at me, a simple Raven
　above the door
Always like a female to have men yelling,
　— though quite unusual to be yelling at a
　Raven above your door
　　　　　　Quoth I, the Raven, "Nevermore."

And of course he began to cry, with ripples of
　sobs and sighs
His frustration got the better of him as he lay
　upon the floor
And though I wished to leave, it was still too
　cold to flap my wings
So I stayed upon that ledge above the door, only
　to hear him mutter,
"Take thy beak from out my heart, and take thy
　form from off my door"
　　　　　　Quoth I the Raven, "Nevermore."

And eventually I left him sitting, for I could not
　help but feel pity
For the sad creature that sat in a slump below
　me on the floor.
So out the window I flew, but when I left I
　already knew
That he would sit there blundering for hours on
　the floor
Sitting there like a baby, stark raving mad on
　the floor.
　　　　　　I decided to talk to humans
　　　　　　　　Nevermore.

Personal Rhythm

i've walked the shadows of my mind
afraid to see what i see in me, and my eyes, and
    my past
but it's not my past that is the fog that curls and
    creeps and poisons
it is the present, and the prospective future
that i breathe in, and choke on, and speak on
until i scream that i'm suffocating and i
    suffocate because i'm screaming
and i ramble, and i talk fast about everything i
    think
but not how i feel, how do i feel? i don't even know
it's all lost in my metaphorical spiral of life
too consumed with sounding unique to be
    unique, and act unique
to at least say how i feel
i feel like a puppet sometimes
with each string in a different hand, of
    schizophrenic puppet masters
pulling me this way and that way
the college way and the work way, for the
    money for the passion
for the satisfaction and the living
how can i keep living like this missing so much
there's always something not there to miss, like
    a brother
who never calls, leaving that empty corridor in
    your heart

that ceases to pump blood, through the veins, to
  the limbs
that are too tired to feel from work and
  rejection and love
and applications and essays and love
full speed, and fuel, no more time for dreams
i used to have so many of, now i dream to
  dream again
to be young again, to not know what i know, to
  not push and push and push
and tear myself apart to know just what is inside
to laugh, and really laugh, from the bottom up,
  not to cover up
a negative feeling jealousy, because she takes me
  over,
wins me over, she beats me over
and steals the things i love to love and grips on
  to those i love
not letting them go, not letting go of the terror
  of being alone
suffering from insomnia because i'm alone at
  night
leaving me tired, i tire so many people out, wear
  them out, try them on
and stretch them out, see if they fit to me, how
  do they work on me,
just how comfortable are they, uncomfortable
  situations are humorous to me
death can be funny to me, so i don't have to face
  the pain, cover up the pain

smile and maybe fool the pain, can't be too
    boring or they won't love me
don't be too plain or they won't like me, impress
    impress impress
get the grade, and get the guy, and hug the
    friend, and talk to god
and smile smile smile, internalize that frown i'm
    told but it's OK to cry
as long as you have it all together
but she writes better and she looks better and he
    talks better and loves better
and she knows better and i can't do any better
and so my mind keeps racing, incoherently
    running, just trying to find a way
to make all the fog and shadows and past and
    present and strings and smiles
STOP

Open Windows

Open windows blast the breeze
Music mocking silent feelings
Night air that the summer wanted
Winter tainted, spring confronted
Made you want me, game I won
Losing forward feelings spun
Car turns fast and red lights warn
Touch me and I start to burn
Searing scorching brakes that scream
You told me once you'd never leave
Driving nowhere always gone
Thoughts of you and start to long
Open windows blast the breeze
Metal crush; scars that bleed
Start to pale with hands outreaching
Through the sirens I hear you speaking
Thought your loss was unsubstantial
Found that you were quintessential
Lost myself within your song
Slipping now, life in your palms
Hope decayed through that music
In your eyes I start to focus
Knowing that the time is slipping
Feeling that your mind is tripping
Open windows blast the breeze
You and I were never real.

Night Swimming

Break into the water, slip faster down
Deep deep deep oblivion
All around me and no where to grasp
Water seeps into my bones
Aqua eyes become my own
And you are fluid still
Lurking somewhere in my motives
You resume swimming through my veins
Thought I was dry dry dry
But am still wet with you
No matter where I turn
You are murky in my vision
Waves tainted with you
Trample, roll, fold into me
Air is no longer
Only your presence filters through
And I drown

Emily wrote at least two versions of this poem; another version follows this page.

Eve

Break into the water, slip faster down
Deep deep deep oblivion
All around me and no where to grasp
Water seeps into my bones
Aqua eyes become my own
And you are fluid still
Build your evening wet with testosterone
To hold my head into the sand
Beckon loves who sew so many scars upon the heart
And leave us to our quiet frustration
I hold my voice inside my throat
Wash my opinions in your disapproving glances
And hear you spit upon my kind
When I am dead, I will not be buried
For my lips had never moved in life
And our story yet untold
Unfolding with the rivers turn
Flowing to those with heart like mine
Loud, but silenced in all your fame
Just for intrinsic differences
Those of us who bleed and bled
Follow with our careful steps
And remain with placid eyes
Those walking dead, who fear to speak
Tremble brave within their soul
In their depart they mark their sacrifice
We are the descendants of Eve, who bit the apple
I cannot swallow down
And leave inside my throat
While I die in the footsteps of Adam

Multiple

Once upon this earth i met you and your eyes
burned a memory of me i could never live up to.
To face you again would be like giving Lucifer a
playground full of innocence with purity swings
and virgin slides waiting to be plucked and
laced with corruption. Like my words muttered
by my father's lips who scorned the day i bled
and became a woman instead of his only girl,
his only girl that he locked inside a prize glass
case until i screamed so loud it shattered all his
expectations. The way this confrontation, this
reinstating of our meeting is shattering your
memory and my sense of worth.

Smoke me until i fill your lungs and dilute your
blood with my fantasies and contradictions.
Fixations that cause obsessions and greed like
that capitalistic tendency to churn out goods
with a price and movement that burns and love
me to prove me wrong to fire that acid inside
and torch. Torch. i may have caused this turmoil
on purpose just to like where i was, told i couldn't
and just enjoy this bliss rambling incoherently
with candles and the only people who could
ever make me feel whole and pure and wanted. i
knew you never wanted me the way i longed for
you and that was the only reason i kept living to
prove you wrong in hopes that you would
smoke me until i filled your lungs.

Mistake

So I read your secrets
Without your permission
And bled your conscience into me
Distilled that liquid poison
Those inner thoughts
Separation numbed to cold

Journey

Crouched beneath the inner child
She held her breath
Inside her hatred
Kills the stardust grip
Glorified in hell
Shunned by holy light
She searches for
Her destiny
Overcome with confidence
She broke the desolate well
And stood above her fears.

Lonely

Understand me
Unlock my mind
And see what possesses
My thoughts
You already know
I hide inside my head
Why don't you
Keep me company.

Indecision

Certain times call for self evaluations
When people press deep down
    Past the grit and grime
And type up
Double spaced biographies
    with bibliographies and footnotes
But I exist in rough draft form
An incoherent free response
That never reaches
(Or doesn't have) a point
It is here that I realize
That I am an expert
    On anything by myself
I could make a thousand assumptions
But their validity
Would be invalid

At night I get glimpses
Moving shadows
    Of what might be inside me
But awake with only obscured memories
Leaving me so thirsty for the truth
That I crave to slit my flesh open
In search of myself
    (I name my razors Lewis and Clark)
Spilling, flooding memories all over my body
And pressing deeper until I find what I am
    looking for
Hold it in my hands, feel its life pulsate
And put it back, content
To know I have finally discovered myself
    (wounds will always heal)

Heaven

In this world of time, a sporadic lapse will send you to another life, so to speak. In one "bleep" of time, your soul will be transported into another body, a body you could have been born into instead of what you were.

In heaven, the souls of unborn children wait to be given life with heavy anticipation. Bodiless life that longs for a form to mold in and belong to. Every three minutes, ten thousand of them are given the right to life. Those ten thousand souls will intertwine until the exact moment of their death — and they will all share that moment.

These souls continue, through each interruptance of time, to travel within and without of each other, facing every condition that life could have given them. Rich, poor, happy, loved, neglected, abused, pampered, tainted — they will experience it all before their shift in this world is up and then return to heaven as used souls. Some to be recycled, some to rest eternally. Only those who have formed into a complete whole, who have learned their meaning, are allowed to stay among the clouds.

And so the helpless souls wander and infiltrate into each other, not knowing what has brought them there. Not remembering that they have lived ten thousand different lives in ninety years, or in ten years, or in twenty years. Only knowing that they have experienced things deep down, and they take the effects of these experiences with them.

Walked This Path

I've walked this path
(Not once) but many times before
The marble slab and concrete
Methodically placed
Under my feet to steady
Under my feet to lead

I've seen the leaves turn color and fall
I've seen the lights turn out
In happy family homes
And yet
I've walked this path
(Not once) BUT MANY TIMES BEFORE

Human Beings

If human beings
Are so inclined
To say just a piece
Of what is on their minds
Once a day
In any way
Maybe they'd be more kind

In our current state
We are homogenous
Lacking the same thing
That you have been denied

You crave it precisely because you
Have been denied it
I reject it because it is something
A man told me to want
And together we have been
Molded transcending those boundaries

Look Inside Myself

If I could look inside myself would I be
    disappointed.
Am I a bad person, do I hate, do I mock, am I
    cruel?
Will I ever be the same?
Am I ever going to understand myself to the
    point where I can explain it to others.
Do I have to tell the world that I am OK.
I know the biggest thing about me is emotion.
I am such an emotional person.
Do others understand the way I operate.
Will they ever, do I?
Confusion is all that comes to mind.
Is it so bad that my most prized possession is
    a tattered notebook and a pen?

My Ideals

I will not change my ideals for you
Wallow in hypocrisy
Just to say I love you
When those words mean nothing
Yet so much at the same time
Like an infant I want to be held
Yet still cry with your arms on me
Longing for that feeling

Blonde

I was blonde
Shall I blame my faults on that
The lust and envy it attracted
Those brunette girls that knew they were more attractive
That black hair that was more inviting
I was blonde, and therefore labeled

Chicken Sub

I ordered a chicken sub
At a small diner
And as I waited
I saw a girl
Of ten
Who was round
Like I was
When I was that age
I watched her
Observe herself
In the dingy cafe mirrors
Already conscious
Of the body faults
She possessed
She caught me looking
And we stared each other down
Thinking
"God, I've been there"
And she thinking
"God, I'll be there"
They called my order
So I thanked them
And left.

I Looked at You

I looked at you with desire
You only saw humor
Laughed at this longing
While I broke inside
Smiled
Then laughed with you to not ruin the mood
I used a knife to heal it
Fire to conceal it
Your ignorance to ease the pain
For this lust
I have nothing
Except your eyes
My broken insides
I looked at you with desire
You look at me with nothing

I Grew in a Time

I grew in a time when nothing was important
No social conflict instilled a passion in the youth
And every movement seemed conquered or fizzled
So we spent our days chasing nicotine and coffee
Complaining about things that didn't really matter
Like the way our daddies looked at us
Or how our mothers forgot to smile
We passed the minutes on our cell phones
And sat on couches with books
Reading about how people were once actually intellectual
I live in a time when nothing is important
My education no longer drives me
My ambition won't come out and play
And every time I try to succeed
I just lie here, and think.

I

I'm on a trip
And I'm alone
And I'm cold
And I don't know
Just where I've been
I take it all in
Fears within
Are talking
While I am walking around
I hear their sound
But not the advice
That they display
I'm alone, tired, don't want to play
These games in names
Of ones I left behind
Reel and roll through my mind
Of experiences that could have been
But will never be
Because of me.

Adolescence

I like to wear
Tangled violets in my hair
A contradiction
Of the blonde innocence
That floats down my shoulders
In inviting curls
That makes men stare
As I walk
Stumbling in platform shoes
That make me feel so special

A Withering Rose

A withering rose
My petals are closed
My scent so sweet
Does no longer exist
Death inevitable
No way to resist
Browning and shrinking
My thorns are dull
Happy memories
Too long ago to recall
It's nothing to avoid
It's no use to cry
At some point in life
We all wither and die.

He Can't Be Alone

HE CANT BE ALONE
Pawns that serve his purpose
Here to move and fall
HE DOESN'T KNOW HIMSELF
Vicarious playthings
We all have one face
HE'S LOST WITHIN A VOID
Familiar for a time
Our purpose was to be discarded
HE'S BROKEN
Pieces of a temporary puzzle
We all fit him once
HE IS A SELFISH CREATURE
Bought the lines he fed us
Love craving consumers
HE MOVED ON
She too will join us soon

He Breathes

He breathes like the ocean
   — calm fury —
And I'm intimidated
By his persona
But love the way he yearns to love me
   With emotional penetration
   And mental stimulation
   Our psychological situation
Remains physical

I swim into his yes
With mermaid grace and cannibalistic intentions
When he looks into the mirror
And only sees traces of me
I know I have won.

Haywire

Secret desires
Exposed too soon
Everything displaced
Haywire
Caught between a wall
And a live wire
Know me
Hold me
But you only let me go
That is all you need to show
Haywire

Have You Wondered

Have you ever wondered
What makes waves break
Or where they come from
Is it the pent up rage
Beneath the surface
Where unseen demons lie
Until the innocent
Are thrust into the open
Taking one last breath of air
As they descend
In a violent crash
Taking down the weak
Along with their misery
As they seep into the earth
Only to return
To their sea
Which causes their pain

Tones

Give me some familiar tones
Shades of grey
        And white
                And black
We all say words
    Speak tongues
Spout endless streams of
Consciousness
But that's all they are
Words
        Syllables
  Sounds
They are on our souls
        Thoughts
  Beings
Move me with your rhythm
        Mind
  And Presence.

Feline Part II

His fangs sank deeper as I struggled
Tried to talk but those animals only growled
Filled with intrinsic knowledge and learned behavior
I never ceded,
But he forced me down
What girls are cats with panther-like men
That claw our individuality and eat our flesh away
Burning in a sun created by males
And maintained by women.

Shades of Purple

Shades of purple
enclose you as you dream
you fake awake
and seem to slip through her
you care about her
in a way you never felt before
the emotional force penetrates deeper than ever
to walk away
would be so easy
but you can't break her
again
you can't bear to break her
again
she shatters so easy
she loves you so deeply
she is your favorite
shade of purple

Entrapment

A boy
Sitting alone
In a corner
His eyes dart
Peruse the room
His hand twist
Into a knot
Turning his knuckles
White
His hair
Uncombed
His clothes
Dirty
No one
Notices
No one
Cares to either
Except
The girl
Sitting alone
In the opposite corner

Emotionally Anorexic

Flying high above your morals
I'm free from your standards
You can't beat me down with your harsh tongue
Your disapproving eyes
Consume me before you let your taste buds feel me
Too hungry for your own good
You can't savor anything
Rushing through the sweetness
Leaving only bitter memories
It's so painful for you to learn
That I will not be digested
Into a mindless, brainless
Creature for you to feed upon

Denial

Too scared to enter
I reluctantly stand
Caught between innocence
And what I think is right
Smothered with morals
Cross held in hand
Emotions all but leading
In the death of me tonight.

I walked in too soon
To stop what could've been
Caught with my reluctance
And frightened by the sight
Covered with sadness
Jaw held in hand
Their emotions all but leading
In the death of me tonight.

Consume

Consume immensely
Build about me
Like wild skin
From winds yet loved
Days stagger off
With slender glass bouquets
That blossom tongue
Only after secret
Songs are sung
I shower books that
Smell like summer
Leave cracked bruises
And slices of myself

Confusion is a Rainstorm

Confusion sweeps over like a rainstorm
When I kiss you and he's in the background
I'm trying to convince my heart
To follow my arms
Lips
Eyes
But your memory is instilled in my mind
Like a bad childhood experience
And I still get flashbacks
Of the way you never loved me
I'm drowning in swirling emotions
Of the affection I never had
And the happiness I possess
Afraid it's all going to go away
Leaving me stranded
In the oblivion of loneliness

Closure

Honey I'm getting up this time
No longer will you keep me down
Embedded in your fury
While you wallow in your rage
I'm wanting to save you from yourself
But you left me no other way
Than to shed your chains and escape
I am barely saving myself; I cannot save you too
Grasping, Craving, Longing, for your selfish
hate to disappear
Something wicked from your insides grow
And to the others it does not show
But to me you are transparent
And I see the hollowness that is present where
your heart should be
And with my rising power I'm no longer lying
at your feet
I'm standing, raising
Rising high above
You
It's fun to see you cower with such fear below
As I saunter away with clear conscience
You'll never take another's innocence
I'm only left with the regret
That I did not tear myself away sooner
I let you permeate my blood cells
And travel to the deepest depths of my mind
Only there do you still reside

And maybe in time the alcohol will fade that too
And the scar on my heart will be the only
memory of you
Besides the faded pictures
In the shattered frames
Packed and gone and strewn away
Goodbye sweetheart, I hope my memory stays
well within your mind
I know you won't forget me, you are the
revengeful kind
But oh no baby you can't hurt me anymore
Your love's succulent victim huddled
in the doorway

Christ

I finger the medallion around my neck
So St. Cecilia can protect me from my sins
Judas to my friends
Stained glass window illuminates
Passes the light of God right through me
Like angel sighs
When I can't seem to be good anymore
Children frightened
Trembling hands
"Make your first confession to cleanse yourself"
As if seven year olds are really that evil
How can I profess my deeds
To shadowed faces
Who never care to know
Mind or matter of a woman
That man reading praying so intently
Never hugged his son
But devotes time to the father
Ironic trinity that puzzles me
For he reminds me of a ghost
And I try to remember
Just when it was that I lost all conviction
Grasp it back
Try to find
But the incense distorts my vision
With its poison smoke
And chokes my lungs with defining scent
As that bell rings for the third time
My punishments are offered up to a Christ
That terrified me from the wall, womb, and soul.

Chocolate Aphrodisiac Poison

Chocolate aphrodisiac poison
Lust hungry little boy
Moving with lethargy
Halcyon eyes
He can shatter with the best of us
For he is glass to me
11:57 and still no rush to end the day
    11:58 and still no words to describe the pain
        11:59 and still more time to live in vain
Midnight and Still
Midnight and Still,
   Still
Orange scents sweep the air
Makes him turn his head again
He lost the trail of me
   Appealing rhythmic kisses —
A mouth that is not mine
Eyes that do not stain

Iridescent oil slicks
Make movements illuminate
In the cliche black of night
We lost him with the purple vapors
Once his eyes ventured into all that I
   could not provide
And I do not weep, but smile
With one last look at my failed endeavor

Catholicism

Knees aching
She continues to pray
Knuckles white
So tightly they bleed
For her sins
She repents today

Faith strong
But does God exist
Accusing stares
The glares they burn
Compassion
Was what she missed
Lips moving
In emotional vows
God's verse
Her curse, she knows
Rosaries
Can't save her.

Faith

Clouds block my way to Heaven
As I repeatedly report
It does no good
Condemning no one
But myself
For the look in your eyes
I wish I were something I am not
I wish I actually was
What you saw in me.

Candles

Your disapproving eyes
Slowly look this way
Can you feel the fire in my presence?
Come too close and I'll ignite you
Burning you with every smile
Charring you with every glance
Dancing in the flames I only want you to join me
I never knew I could hurt this much
Like a moth singed by the flame
I see your wings withdraw with pain and curiosity
Fly around me
Test the boundaries
See just how far you will go
How far will you go
Before you're dancing in my embers
Breathing through the cinder
We all turn to ashes sooner or later
Sooner or later
fly and dance with me
fly and burn with me
Two hearts melting into one
We all turn to ashes sooner or later
Come too close and I'll ignite you
Come closer
we'll weld into one
We all turn to ashes sooner or later

Blue Lips

Blue lipped girl said she lost her ambition
When you move her like that
Jealous of your purpose
Envy all your reason
Bite
this
down
now
Sway
in me
Dark like — your eyes
Move — like the light
Lie — about your depth
Scream
Scream
The skyline marked it
Blue cloud rolling
Something burning in this passage
Blistered
Her body
Cold
And barren
Static
Move it
Move it
Now
Please
Hurt, it hurts, eyes are alive
Even though the lips are blue

Black Pearl

Saw the black pearls
You draped around my neck and screamed
Be beautiful for me
Silent whispers break like waterfalls
June invades my mind
Invades my mind with color
Dripping canvas stains that bleed like honey
I was never good enough for you
Shatter all that is familiar
Rip the sea into fragments
Are you afraid of what unearths you from a
 dream?
And leaves you in your plain reality
Sweaty palmed and white faced
Bones that lay like liquid patterns late at night in
 bed
Without me
A girl with my face that lacks my humor
You clutch her now while I sing:
"See I was once a black pearl
On your string of white, such an innocent color
Imperfection to the very last drop"
But I lost my faith when I was only sixteen
So love her like you would once have loved me
If I was still a black pearl
In your possession
Harmony flows into your ears
My lyrics will make love to you again
When you recover from your bitter-sweetness
You find me,
Only a whisper in the shadows
On a string of black pearls

Beneath the Down

I am beneath the down
A creature of something unknown
Masked to those numb in their cubicles
Void of depth and trying to tell me they cannot
    perceive
Folds below my mind tell me they will not
Because it is hardly ever a matter of "can"
Scorned for sitting in the posture of a man
But praised in ideas lacking of estrogen
Maybe these unconscious hollows hated Mary

On the eve of my intentional descent
I was normal and composed
A pseudo-perfect exterior
But clawing wild hysterical
Wrapped in Ginsberg
Trying to grasp a religion that I did not
    understand
Picturesque, Middle-class, Spoiled youth
Stereotype that was driving me insane
Pulling out the follicles and pieces of my brain

People said I had only left to fall under
But after tumbling I find
I am beneath the down.

Aurora

To Aurora
The child unborn
The embryo yet to be conceived
May you know
    This name is strong
    Chosen carefully
    Marked and destined
The way they said I was
    Female Cain
    Removed from sin
    To bear you.

May you love
    The way I have loved
    The way I was loved
Those who broke me
    Saved me too
And no mother could deny that
    To Aurora
    The prodigal daughter
Yet to venture in this world
    May you defy what is known
    And prove the untrue
May you accomplish what I have failed to do.

Sit by the Window

As I sit by the window
A cool breeze hits my back;
Sending me into
A chilly daydream
Of a time, when I was rain
I, like the crystal drop,
Descended from a gray cloud
Upon an unblossomed rose
Over time, I seeped below the soil
And into the roots,
And the flower and I made a bond.
I helped it live, and helped it grow
While it gave me a meaningful existence
And then, one sunny day
Its petals begun to spread,
Openly, beautifully,
So that no one could not stop
And look in its direction.
Yet, while bees came to smell
The sweet pollen and humans gaze
At the pretty sight
No one thought of the rain that fell
From a dirty cloud
That had helped it grow
And one day, a gardener
Came and cut the rose,
His shears crisply cut through us,
The rose and I

Separating us forever.
But I know that I still am
In some parts of my crimson friend,
Deep within her
Hidden from everyone
And so I still live on,
In the petals of a rose
As I ascend to my cloud
Wondering what's going to happen
The next time I fall.

As I Look Around

As I look around
I become frustrated
Will the people
Ever know just
How deeply I think
And feel
And hurt
Will they ever even try
Will they break down
My defenses
And storm into my soul
To break me down and dissect me
Understand me
Feel me
Will they look at my
Beating heart
And watch it rise and fall
While it pushes blood
Through my weak body
Pushing through the
Blood
And bone
And organs
Will they ever see my soul
Or am I just a waste
Of their time.

Built by Nature

I was built by nature
(supposedly — according to the experts)
To be strong in composure
But weak in independence
I denied this.
Perhaps by pure defiance
Or influence from the womb
I sought to be strong in mind
In emotion
In value.
So I shone
Felt that liberation
And then you —
Of the opposite sex
I was taught to fear and mistrust
To let you in would be my downfall
But you were different
And I succumbed to it
I know not whether
I have gained or lost
I can justly say, however
I was built by nature to struggle
For the same independence
Held by any man.

We Live Not for Ourselves

We live not for ourselves
We die not for ourselves

But here I am by myself
In this house
Too vacant to pray
But too full to not be offended

>   Become the body
>   And the blood

Become something I am not
Not worthy of salvation
I hear them speak directly to me
And shut out
What I can't admit
Altars repel with beauty

>   Who takes away the
>   Sins of the world

But mine were too heavy to take
Hopeless sinner
Thoughtless prayer
Void redemption
Lust for forgiveness

>   Only this I want
>   But to know the Lord

Bliss

Bliss
Word that strikes those vocal cords
Vibration
Of the purest kind
Kiss Kiss
To make the sweetness sour
Live
To make me pure

Brushstrokes

Compare me to her
Like I'm some moldable form
Muted and mumbled
Incoherent thunder tornado
And she won't bring herself to speak
Shout your red at me
Like I'm her canvas toy
Bleach myself with paint like hers
And soak into your permanence.

Friend Poems

Stop Until the Evening Starts

Stop until the evening starts
Die among with falling leaves
Sleep within the heart of me
One day you might be saved
Say you love her twice and leave
Forgotten never
Forgive me still
Among winds that fail to cede
Lovers lie in dusted faces
Bad mood junkie
Starts to say
"Once we're grown, it's all for shit"
And I've tried to slice it once today

You try to tell yourself it's just a razor burn
That wounded flesh
Painted pins and reds
Starting to form the
Blue in your eyes melts to
Grey sky when you see me
Here you lie to
Face me when I cut my
Legs that walk haunt me in my
Dream that you can read my
Mind wanders, always feeling
Something bothers my disposition
Daily I pour out my soul to
You ignore the constant plea
Asking myself to stop the pain
You try to tell yourself it's just a
Razor burn upon my leg

Summertime of Innocence

Fragile Minds that intertwine
Throughout the years we sat
Soaking up the memories
Taking for granted what was given
Right in front of our eyes
Not blind, but in denial
To notice we were changing
Childish dreams of loves unbroken
So many nights words gone unspoken
We were the innocents we so strive to be

Trampoline Kisses sour with time
Like warm Kool-Aid in the summer
Our souls once the ingredients
Now spoiled beyond drinking
Separated by the differences we cannot
    overcome
The dreamers with the lovers
The sinners with the dreamers
The lovers with the fighters
We all came from the same bright day

Fighting past the pain
Searching for the love
Holding us all together
We were the innocents we so strive to be

12 Cigarettes to Freedom

window down
light me up
music loud
night air cold
green light says
push the gas
drive far
no return
window up
sweater on
bags in back
cash in pocket
window down
light me up
life behind
us ahead
red light lies
push the gas
window up
music louder
three more hours
window down
light me up
then they'll know
push the gas
we'll be gone
window up
sweater off
music slow
drive through food
windows down

light me up
one more hour
green light says
push the gas
cross the border
window up sweater on
music drowning
now they'll know
sun arising beds are empty
window down
light me up
money wasted
red light lies
push the gas
now we're gone
life is changed
window up
no, back down
now light me up
anxious girls
worried parents
green light smiles
push the gas
window up
sweater off
music loving
change in back
no shower
still like the smell
window down
light me up
can't find us now
red light lies

push the gas
light me up
keep on going
light me up
now we're happy
light me up
away from everything
light me up
I found paradise
with window down
music loud
now light me up

Unreachable

You sit there
Lost in your own world
Moving to independent rhythms
And I watch you
Intently
I'm bleeding from the inside
On opposite corners
Opposite minds
Loneliness is tearing away
My insides
Everything I want
Everything I need
Your sugar smiles
Penetrate the fragileness
Of my heart —
Your heart
Intangibly intertwining
In the silence
Of the fury
You pay no attention
To the translucent emotions
I am sending
As I cry
The sour tears
For the breaking of our being

We

A group of dreamers sat together
Sifting through their heads
Poured out the glitter and rust they held inside
Thought back to the days they were all so alike
Cannons caught in the nightmare of suburban
　　life
Ready to be shot into the world
Ready to be seen
They would make it all together
They all would make their dream
To outrun the pain
To outlive the lie

We Had Eight Eyes

We had eight eyes and four minds
That we welded into one
And he said
"We always have tomorrow"
But deep in our hearts
We knew it wasn't true
For tomorrow held futures
And unhappiness
What we had was this hour
This minute
We had our eight eyes and four minds
In one galaxy
Staring down the world
With coffee and cigarettes
Because if it wasn't the world that killed us
At least the nicotine would

We Traded Childhoods

We traded childhoods, it seemed
With those sweet songs
Like poison
That tainted our heads with fantasy
Maybe they didn't break my innocence
But they certainly contributed to my delinquency
Thank you dearly for sharing with me your mentor
We are the disciples of things we could not have understood then
But follow with fervor now
Lyrics that molded
And melodies that guided
We swapped them like baloney and peanut butter sandwiches
Mothers never can get your favorite right when they have more than one child
We traded memories
With those songs, those psalms, those heartbeats
I never did understand you until then.

You Glanced at Me

You say you glanced at me
Driving
When you knew I couldn't look back
Afraid of my eye contact, steady
Unsteady me
Driving you
What an ironic situation
She's in the backseat
In your mind
But I'm driving
I thought I was driving
— You saw me driving? —
But she's in the backseat
[Like always]
Glances, judgments, wishes
Decipher yourself, I can't anymore
Unsteady me
I am only driving you
Driving
Though she's in the backseat
Glaring
One eye on each of us
Pretty petty innocent pretty girl
Riding
She was only riding
You glanced at me
While I was driving
She and you
Riding
I thought I was driving
You both were riding
Maybe we all were

When I Recall a Trampoline

My darling sweetheart
You have left me cold
Where was your promise of warmth?
Timid, misunderstood boy
Spiky intentions and wounded hair
Bilingual with your sexuality
And yet there still was no room for me
But I will always understand
And never question
"What scared you when you were little?"
No need to speak,
Your darkest secret I do know
I heard Lucifer whisper your name
And smacked him in disgust
For no creature should be able to speak your
Words in vain;
I will comfort through my hurt
And give you my life
Give you my life
Darling you have left me happy
Though lacking your embrace
I can still look at you every day
Speak into you
Seep into you
If I can do those things
I can bleed for you
The most beautiful creation
You will always be inside me

We Were Young Once

We were young once
With alterna-rock on our radios and dirty
    thoughts inside our heads
That we were ashamed to think
But you were tangible and made me feel normal
Grew up by only your support
Putting the lid on my psychotic tendencies
That would have left scars on me somewhere
When you moved I thought I would lose
    everything
But with our distance I felt even closer in your
    words
That spoke directly to my heart
And made me feel like a cheesy adolescent

Now we are mature, they say it anyway
Though I don't know if it is true
Because you still listen to that alternate rock
And I still think those dirty things
But you are now intangible
While I am beyond normalcy, with scars that
    are pink and deep

The Light Beams

You used to shine
Lying on the blanket
Only the light beams live there now
And wrinkled socks I found underneath the bed
I wear them on my feet but they slide right off
I cannot hold them:
   Your feet held them better

And so the socks go ownerless
I take down the pictures of you
As I chase the light beams, I wonder if
My picture still has a home on your refrigerator:
   I guess our love was always cold.

I'm missing a left sock
As I waltz around the room
Carefully removing your key off my key-chain
It is big and gold and heavy
Seeming to make my petite, silver keys
Inadequate to unlock any door:
   Your Heart was always dead-bolted anyway.

As dead flowers and cards
Get cozy inside the trash can,
I chase the light beams
Warming my face — they mock me
I can feel their presence but they are impossible
   to grasp:
   Intangible dreams.

      They used to make me so happy.

Talula

Her eyes glow darker than mine
    And her talent more apparent
I, too, see the stares she knows she receives
But brushes aside
By painting a faint blush upon her cheeks
Hiding behind an aura of naïveté
    Her random actions methodically placed
She says, she swirls, blurs, distorts
She talks of illusions
    Delusions
But she is clear, and plain, and normal,
"I am drowning in this misery of mine," she
    casually moans,
Hinting for the tone of troubled artist
    So I roll my eyes again
And immediately become the villain
    Sinister and self directed
Leaving her the princess
Vulnerable and radiant
And a magnet for me to repel
But she tries to flip
Flip flip
    Us over again
Stuck Stuck Stuck together
And I can't escape our bind
But forever, I am tainted knowing
That her eyes glow darker than mine.

Sister

Why must you distort things
So they fit into your nice tidy
Four squared box of self denial
You forget you tasted Lucifer once
Like me
I finally decided I could never be like you
Now you're livid because I stopped trying

On the Shelf

I've been put back on the shelf again
One friend with dynamic beauty
The other classic poise
I stand, barely
Blonde? Breasts I know aren't firm
I'm pretty
In the right light occasionally
Never pitied those mermaids
Those sisters whose scales began to decay
Underwater
Yet they never let themselves drown

Reading fairy tales,
I always wondered why the heroines
    were prettiest
When they were asleep and quiet
So I tried to open my mouth
To achieve something I'd never been
    allowed to see
I've been put back on the shelf again.
Never could find that happy medium
Between too simple and too complicated
So why am I content
Upon this cliff, for speculation
Throw the judgments in my direction
Maybe only I can handle them
Could this be the reason
I've been put back on the shelf again

Robots

Have you realized we have begun to think alike
Because we share this room
Day after every other day
Unknowingly conforming to what we
    Are taught to believe
For if we realized it
We would rebel
Wild
That someone smacked our little hands
    From which we withdrew and obeyed

Secretly our minds fused
Into one beating intellect
Talking from twenty-four mouths
And forty-eight eyes
With hundreds of steel teeth
That bite
With vigor

Conformed to what I know
    (what we know)
Is that we are now Robots
And didn't even notice
The flesh dripping away
To echo our metal reflections

Maybe

Maybe
You just called
Cause you were bored
And no one else was home
So you'd just see what's going on
Maybe
You just called
Cause you were thinking
And no one else consumed you
But me and my being
Maybe
You just dialed
Without thinking or caring
And having to look up my number
Maybe
You just dialed
For the thousandth time
And finally got the nerve to follow through
Maybe
You don't care
Cause you belong to someone else
And we weren't meant to be
Maybe,
Just maybe, God made you just for me.

Magnetic

Sister burning full and blue
Said she cracked your bruise again
Secret dirty stagger smells
Away like evening avenue
Pronounce a tongue like love for teaching
Wild bouquet slender wind
Not a song — only shower glass
Have blossoms to tendril skin
Summer mornings leave dark liquid
Slice up pages people grow
Through dry want
Will you build red minuets
To pass away the Prozac pill

Picnic

Hollow I am to you
Emptied from the inside out
You lay naked in the field
Like a dead body sunbathing
I walk carrying oranges
  — only two —
Followed by a black mouse
Who scurries and stops
Scurries and stops
Grass that towers to your torso
And breezes to your feet
I lay next to you as you seem to
Not notice
But take one of my oranges to eat
Unpeeling my peel
I throw a piece to little black mouse
And he eats intently
You bite slowly
And let the juice dribble down your chin
But withdraw away from me
When I try to wipe it off
Black mouse starts to sleep
As I lay upon my back
You finish the orange and discard it over your
    shoulder
Almost as indifferent as your love for me

Let Me Go

They say that every picture tells a story
Is that the reason why
My captured image looks happy?
You have me right where you want me
Caught between
Dependency and resistance
Please, let me go
I'm my own person
Let me feel my independence
Let me leave your condescending tones
You are not my superior, nor I your inferior
It's not that I don't need you
But I've learned to walk
Without the use of your hands
I've learned to talk
Without the use of your words
Even though your thoughts influence
Please let me go
I can stand on my own two feet
And I know your body
Is tired and worn
Tear down this wall
I am forced to stay behind
The gate is locked and far too high to climb
Please let me go
Of the restraints I gave myself to so willingly
For I didn't know
Just how tight you would make them

Let me go
Don't think I won't sink to desperate measures
To get out of this place
I have to leave
Don't be sad, in my heart I carry the sweet memories
Of your beautiful face
Of your grace
Of all your love
Of all your strength
But please
Just let me go
So I can miss you

Just Lie Next to Me

Just lie next to me
Don't do anything but breathe
Because I know what you think by the rhythm
   of your breath
And we can lie in silence
With our innocence
And melt into the sheets with time
My standards die when I look into your eyes
And everything I have ever known has ceased to
   be true
So just lie next to me
And don't expect my sacrifice
Let them think we're sexual
While we wax intellectual
Talk of our inhibitions
Laugh at our indiscretions
Time stops to envy our situation
While we just exist
Fall in love
And just lie next to me

Is It the Way?

Is it the way
I'm not afraid
To contradict you
Or admit when
I like something weird
The way I freely
Break all your rules
Or wear my pajamas
To a black tie affair
Or walk barefoot
While everyone else
Straps shoes on
Or the way
I inquire about your mind
When all others
Tell you to keep quiet
The way I
Write poetry in the
Midst of a raging party
Because a sentence
Evoked a song
The way I
Open my mind
To things others are
Afraid to seek
Is it the way
I laugh at nothing
Or cry at everything
Is it the way I like you
That makes you
Want to be around me.

I Could Paint This on Glass

I had an epiphany
But you just rolled your eyes at me again
Is it because I sparked something
That lit you burning, fuming outward
(I annoy you and your senses sometimes)
Or is it because I will make something of myself
And you don't believe that you ever could

I tried to slow to an agreeable pace
But you halted, completely stopped and thought
   about the life
Growing in the hungry wombs of our friends
The thought of motherhood never seared as
   deep into me
(Even though my stomach growled just as loud
   as yours)
So I kept on moving
And maybe I never stopped to let thought
   sink in

I will become what I set out to be
But you refuse to set out for anything
Only ebbing away at my confidence
Propelling me raving, jealous away from you
(We never could be content)
And I was a fool to think a bond between
   two girls
Would follow us into womanhood

I am not an inward being
But you are anything but external
Eventually I realized
The large wounded eyes just don't work on me
    anymore
(Like hollow marbles)
You always said I was so talented
And I could paint this on glass if I wanted to.

Heather Says

Heather says
She wants to be held at night
By the man who loves her
She wants to wake up
And be too occupied
To answer the phone
Heather says
She wants to wear
His shirt
While she cooks
Chocolate chip pancakes
On a rainy Sunday morning
Heather says
All she wants
Is love.

He Listens

He listens
But does not understand
The words she says
His ignorant nature
Leaves him bewildered
As she speaks from her soul
The words that she is using
The nature in her tone
Leave him utterly confused
Like a puppy he sits and stares
He wants to comfort but he does not know how
She spills her heart
Her mind, her soul
Her mangled body
Cries and sobs
And he finally understands
What she is saying
But all too late.

He

"He's only a boy,"
She tried to tell me
But I couldn't get past his eyes
Deep like mine
I meet him in the desert, dry
We talk about our thirsts and hungers
Her voice is in my head
"He's only a boy,"
But in this moment, he is my twin
Sand blows and we feel nothing
He touches my hair
Then I feel everything
"He's only a boy,"
Our laugher echoes for miles
Regrettably, it catches her ear
In minutes she is in front of us
Pulling me, killing me
"He's only a boy."
"He is my twin."
To her, our desert is wrong
I ride with her, away
And feel emptiness for the first time.

Glass Prisoner

He laughs and his head tips back
His hair falls carelessly past his eyes
That sparkle like rain in the sun
Protruding a sound of happiness
From his gut and out his mouth
His hand then reaches up and touches her face
Ever so gently
His brown windows look deep into
Hers of blue
And break
These two can never be together

Girl

Girl, we lie like strangers
In this room we have occupied one thousand times
Still, in the dark that you believe is not only external
Permeates our souls as well
I never thought we would experience this type of informality
But tonight we lie like strangers
And I feel nothing but empty.

Friendships

Friendships bleed with color
Mother says it's all a phase
And hands will clench with youth
Innocence is stripped away
With experiences
We were never meant to feel
Heather will always wax philosophical
While Kerry and Priya
Make a Starbucks quest
I hid the emotion felt while years unfold
But leave my name upon the papers
Teachers will always hold
To say they knew me
Trampoline truth or dare
That will live in infamy
With the healing scars
Late night procrastination
On the phone with the drama king
I love yous and I love yous and the one
"I love you" that never meant anything
Lynne says it tastes like strawberries
Breaking of the world
And molding into another
We all said we'd never be right again
But Mike said he wouldn't forget and
Jenni can't forget
Tequila misadventures when
Kerry fell off the bed
Music voiced the feelings
We didn't know we were allowed to feel
And we all looked at the purple moon
To lead us into life

Splint

Mark your orange and red
With my spectrum of purple kisses
Our innocence slipped away like melted
    ice cream
Running to our elbows
While you ran across the sea
Left me here to fend alone
I sparked the moment I knew I loved you
And watched it fizzle to the ground
Sister burning blue candles to match the
    sadness in your eyes
Apart we sliced the fractured bone
To mend within our skin
As one speaking soul that screams
We died when you blew out the candles.

Day Dreaming

Day dreaming
Of you and I together
We sit so contently in each other's arms
You're strumming at your guitar
While I mindlessly scratch at paper
Your melody
My lyrics
Slowly becoming one
We become a song
You know me by the look in my eyes
And I brush the hair out of your face
To look at you
Deeply
Past the skin
You gently take my hands, guiding them on
  your guitar
Trying to teach me a chord
And your touch makes the sun feel cold
You reflect on my poetry
My peace of mind
And we laugh
At our flaws and imperfections
Slowly time passes
I fall asleep in your arms
I can only hear your heartbeat
Only see your eyes
I am content until I awaken
To find you were my daydream

An Ode to Him

I'm looking for your replacement
    Another warm body
To pretend they will protect me
From hearts such as yours
I'm looking for more
Blank eyes
    And hollow words
I crave so deeply
        A non-existent love
To make me feel
Complete
If only for a moment
So I won't have to
    Admit to myself
        To yourself
        To everyone

    That live in your memory
A nightmarish photo album
    Of tears I never cried

We were too bland for that

Abstracted Thoughts

Abstracted thoughts
That form inside
Your adolescent mind
Do not sit right with me
And your bitterness
Does not show
   To any of the others
But I taste it in the air
Whenever you are near
   Bear with me darling
As I struggle to regain my balance
On a planet without you

An Ode to a Nameless Someone

I see you across that glass
With my arms outstretched I see my reflection
almost touch you
But the closer I walk towards you
The further your reflection seems to be
Decaying in front of me
I remember summer and the heat it added to us
Scents of my orange peels and your cigarettes
Still linger on my clothes
You introduced me to the fact that I could feel
I exposed you to the fact you could be so much
more than what you were
You were so new to me
And despite your past, I was so different to you
We lit up rooms that summer
We lifted spirits that summer
Us partners in crime and passion and fun and
ridiculousness
And I knew I couldn't be young forever
But I could never be old enough for you
I was lost in your excuses and your
it doesn't matters
While you carried me around
With indifference
We both ignored the fact that we were wrong
And now I'm stuck in this rut
Thinking of you
While you're laughing

Not thinking of me
And you're loving
Not thinking of me
And your living
Not thinking of me
You continue your existence with all
your false authority
And programmed goals that you refuse to admit
I have instilled in you
Did you push me out of your subconscious or
did I ever sleep there?
At least I know I will grow out of this
And I won't think of you
But when you get there
You will think of me
And when you see the color purple
You will think of me
And when your heart gets broken
You will think of me
And every time you catch the scent of oranges
You will think of me

Alice

Extend my arm
So I can see
Just where the wounds have started to heal
Didn't like it
So we tried to cut it off
Us crazy
Separate yet connected
And you brought me purple band-aids
To patch up any indiscretion
That day I loved you deeper
Than I ever thought I could
So sear this bond
Metallic and heavy
With tequila and a little bit of blood
We'll bake chocolate bread by the sewer
And maybe I'll throw up that chicken sandwich
But you'll make sure my senses stay intact

Void direction
We drove like liquid
To places we had never been
Always wanting to wrap ourselves
Back up into that perfect package
Perfect tongue
Couldn't keep my truths from you
So I called you Alice
To give the definition you deserve
And maybe you called me Chloe
To mock my lack of sweetness

Broke the boys that said they loved us
Those that we loved had broken our souls
Only felt whole when I was with you
Fitting comfortably like the perfect pair of socks
Not white
But black
Our petty preferences
No one else would get
You found love but you don't like it
I found love but won't admit it
And maybe we should just give up
To save everyone some time

So now we're faced with tangible separation
Real and ominous
To where I want to tear the calendar off the wall
Tears that do not fall, but form within my body
And make it hard to walk
Who will hold that razor still?
Leaving with the strength we've gained
Loving with the heart we've trained
And maybe I can't see your face
But you'll always be Alice to me.

Incoherence

When he is far away
Which is always
I feel I am not whole
I see my body as one
And my face as one
But do not feel them as one
I see my reflection and think
"That is not me"
This blur of blonde and blue and green
I feel me as purple cycles
Moving with a rhythm that is not his but mine
And while I am far away
He feels himself in me
With a hybrid of blues and green and purples
Because warmer colors are too hot to wear
So in our minds
We committed sin
And in the room of my innocence
We committed sin
I said, I want the door shut
Because it was open
And if the door was open, I was not me
I know I am, and I know he is
So therefore the door had to be shut
So we could exist
But it was open.
So does this mean I am not me but him
And he not him but me
If the door is shut?

Family Poems

Marjorie

Sometimes I pretend I'm you
And place your hairclip
Rusting in its home on my shelf
Into my mane and watch how
It sparkles, radiates a unique beauty
But is chipped and cracked on one side
And I wonder
How did you wear it?
In your hair like mine
High or low?
On what occasion?
It could never match your eyes
They say are mine
Or mine or yours
So determined and driven towards an unseen
spectrum
And what dress did it match?
On a body like mine
Was it a present?
From the alcoholic whom you booted
From your door
To raise three little girls alone
They say you dreamed
So many dreams like mine
Dreams I am left to fulfill alone
Dreams that couldn't be met
In a world like yours
And can only be satisfied

In a world like mine
So accepting of powerful femininity
When I was little I talked to air
And they heard your voice
In a voice like mine
Only stronger and clearer and more apparent
I guess we are connected
By a name like mine
But isn't it ironic
In that small gap of time
We missed each other entirely?
So I put the hairclip, my fantasy of you
back on the shelf
And form back into my separate person
Noble person?
Person not able to exist without you before me
But still I stare
At your reflection
So similar to a reflection like mine.

Protector

Protector
You sheltered this dream
This vision
This yellow haired imp
And gave me happiness mixed with comfort
So I reached as high as you told me I could
Still haven't yet grasped what you seem to know
    I will find
Protector
You sheltered this dream
This vision
This yellow haired imp
And gave me happiness mixed with comfort
So I reached as high as you told me I could
Still haven't yet grasped what you seem to know
    I will find
Protector
You are behind and underneath
Supporting this girl
This woman
For eternity
Protector
Never weak
You cleanse the wounds with your songs
And fight away demons with your smile
Protector,
You are my best friend
You are my mother.

To Daina

When I was born into your world
You took me under wing
I was your pet, your doll, your toy,
I was the coolest thing.
Then we grew a little more
I opened up my mouth
It seemed that you had found
A little enemy in the house
So we had our differences
Had our share of fights
We said those mean and hateful things
(We both still claim we were right)
And then we hit that turning point
I think it's safe to say
That we grew mature enough
To talk from day to day
From that talk we grew this bond
From this bond I grew a friend
And from this friend I grew a sister
Plus a brother, and a nephew, and a nephew
once again
And now I look at you with your children
And feel a love that is no other
For while you love me like a sister should
You also love me like a mother
So happy mother's day to you
Even though I'm not your daughter
I love you like a sister
And I love you like a mother

Teresa's Sickness

She looked so frail
Curled in fetal position
Blankets enveloping her being
With diagonal folds
Like some classic Greek statue
Of a dying goddess
Looked as if she'd break
If I breathed
So any breath was so still
And I cried
Out of selfish neglect
And the thought
Of what if this was
Real.

And days when I am
Distempered from stress and
Lack of sleep, I think only
Of my mother and how
She is the only person
Who can truly make me happy.
What will I ever do when that angel leaves
This world?

People Tell Me

People tell me
To not be like you
Including yourself
But it's hard to
Not want to be you
So strong and independent
You stand by yourself
You are beautiful,
And you flaunt it
But so would I
If I were you
Your large demanding eyes
Take control of me
As your delicate face speaks words
That are comical in a way
You're everything
I want to be
You're everything I'm not
You're my only sister
The only one I've got
And that's just fine
Because no one compares
To you.

Daina

I've always been loud
I've never been shy
I've never been afraid
To look you straight in the eye.
Always straightforward
Never held back
I've never said I'm pretty I don't believe I'm
    right
But if you dared to challenge
I was ready for the right
I'm not self absorbed
Though some say I am
I look out for others as best as I can
I'm not as tough as you
Think.

Terri

In my first year of life my mother has sent me
>away to Pennsylvania
I cry on my aunt's shoulder
Cousin Johnny is jealous of me, and makes my
>life miserable
They say Sharon is just born
And mother can't handle two babies at once
With that man in her house as well
I stare at the mobile above this secondhand crib
And long for Maryland.
I am four and my mother is crying in front of me
For the first — of many — times
She thinks my father didn't come home
But he is lying in the gutter outside
With Sharon still asleep
And Vicki up and gone
I stare at her with big brown eyes
And wish for something I don't understand.
Four birthdays later and I am sleepwalking
I am waking up on the arm of the couch
Not knowing how I got there
My thin yellow pajamas sticking to itchy fabric
>with paste — like sweat
My father fills us with poison
My mother takes it and swallows it down
I stare into this darkness
And hope for daylight.
I am ten years old and seeing a woman's strength
>for the first time

My mother's arms working mechanical
A muscle expanding and contracting as her face
　　stays lit with pride
Cleaning out the bottles and cans from the
　　cupboards
And the ice box — And the drawers — And the
　　couches — And . . .
My father has been told to leave
I don't stare anymore
And we laugh in the kitchen to Three Dog Night.
Ninth grade is beginning and I am joining Vicki
　　at high school
Leaving Sharon in Intermediate
I walk out of the door in the morning, with my
　　mother
We walk up the same path and then turn in
　　opposite ways
There is no car parked in our garage
No money in our wallets
I see the neighbors watch us from the windows
And try not to feel ashamed.
Next year Sharon is joining me
We can't afford dictionaries, encyclopedias, or
　　extra books
So we make do with some old National
　　Geographics
Until our teachers begin to burn out
Claiming they rode torpedos in World War II
Or falling asleep at their desks
I see so many people fighting for things around
　　the world

And our town sleeping through it.
Summer before graduation and mother is remarrying
Vicki is just now leaving for college
Sharon is never home, leaving me the only one to witness
Mom balancing the checkbook, rubbing her head
Carrying in two bags of groceries for the entire month
The wrinkles on everyone's faces
I see the world scoffing at single parent homes
And am mad that ours is now two again.
As a senior, my counselor informs me that our income is low
That I'll never get to college as if I didn't already know
Sharon is trying drugs
Mother is starting to look like some of my teachers
I don't want to go away
But I prepare to be a secretary and marry Larry
I see myself following my mother's footsteps
And am doing nothing to stop it.
Mid twenties and already too bitter
I find all the clues of adultery
And my daughter is sick all the time
I plan to throw Larry out like he was my father
But he leaves in the middle of the night
Like a coward
I see an empty hole
And want my mother and her strength.

My daughter Daina is five years old
We live with my sister and her daughter Valerie
    as well
We struggle like mom
Rose the daycare lady has left Daina on a street
    corner
And Valerie still wets the bed
But we all smile and have sleepovers every night
I see what our lives must look like to outsiders
And I ignore them, we are happy and full of love
    — but something must give soon.
Twenty-eight and still a secretary
A man comes in every day with wrinkled shirts
    and tired eyes
I see the weight of divorce on him
I know how he feels
So we begin to exchange stories of our children
And our troubles and our exes
I feel something I've never felt before
And I know that it is contentment.
1982 my mother is dying of brain cancer
Such an undeserved fate at the end of a long
    hard life
Her long blonde hair has been taken away
I tell her just what she has given to me
I share with her the wisdom and family I have
    gained
I let her know I have never been ashamed of
    anything in my life
I see her die
And the pain is deeper than anything before.

One year later I am being blessed again
Giving birth to a daughter I see has her Nanny's
    disposition and spirit
I can't call her my mother's name so soon, so I
    name her Emily
And put Marjorie in the middle
She will grow without ever knowing my mother
So I will have to fill that myself
I see her stare at me with my mother's eyes
And know this cycle will never stop.

By Emily Cella
Dedicated to my mother and Nanny

As I Read

As I read what I wrote
Replay what I spoke
Redo what I did
Resing what I sung.
I see a pitiful poet
Whose day has come
I think of past days
I dream of past ways
I remember past dreams
I hope for new luck
I see a pitiful poet
Whose mind is caught and stuck
As I reemerge from my mind
Refound what I find
Rerun what I ran
Rewrite what I wrote
I see a pitiful poet
Whose pen never spoke
I think of help from above
I dream of the ones I will love
I remember those I hate
I hope for a new life
I see a pitiful poet
Whose poems never end
I replay scenes
Resaw what I have seen
Redid what I've done
Rewind to the past

I see a pitiful poet
Whose ideas never last
I think of Jay's humor
I dream of Daina's radiance
I remember my soldier
I hope to see him again
I see a pitiful poet
Who is a part of all of them.

Volcano Girl

In my world of black and whites
I remained a placid shade of gray
Guilty of my perfect childhood
I never seemed to fit
Too square around the edges
To share sides with wild siblings
Clashed their bad experiences with my good
And so I sit
Volcano girl
Building timid tensions among the humor gang
Behind my smile I am dying
Stabbed by memories without my presence
They all seemed so happy before I came along
Before I entered the room
Before I dared exist
And so I sit
Volcano girl
Ready to erupt with emotion they just will
never understand
Never try to understand
Never care to understand
I never seemed to fit
This gray volcano girl
In my world of black and whites.

Short Stories

With a Little Guiding Light

A blonde little girl sat alone among the dandelions in her small backyard. The sun shone brightly making her gold highlights shine. Her pigtails blew in the summer breeze as she picked the yellow flowers and stained her chin yellow. Her imagination rapidly expanding, she began to talk to fairies, and laugh amusingly in her own dream world. She was quite content, until two older boys hiding behind the trees began to snicker. Snickering turned into harsh laughter as they cried, "She's out of her mind!" Bursting into tears, she flew inside the house. Up the stairs into the kitchen, jumping into the arms of a beautiful woman with hair just as blonde. "It's OK, honey," she comforted. "You talk to who you want to; imagination is a wonderful thing to have."

A few years down the road, the same girl has entered kindergarten. Smells of paste and animal crackers fill the room as the group of hyper five-year-olds begins to scribble with jumbo crayons on construction paper. While kindergartners lack artistic ability, the blonde child's drawing skills were nonexistent. While the swarms of little boys and girls received a happy sticker for their masterpieces, her drawing was placed in the wastebasket. Once again taking comfort in the arms of the woman with golden hair, the little girl cried, "I can't color like the other kids do!" "Everyone has their talents, sweetie. Why don't you sing for me, I love to hear you sing." Relaxing, the little girl opened her mouth and began to cheerfully hum a song. Within moments, her displeasure subsided as she began to dance around the room.

Now the girl has entered fifth grade. A whole new world of long division and books with no pictures. A world where students begin to discriminate against each other, as society begins to show its toll. Cliques beginning to form simply because a person didn't wear the "right" type of clothing, or listen to the "right" type of music. The girl with golden hair still emerged in innocence; walked over to a child she had known for many years. "Can I sit here?" she asked politely. "No," the child said simply and abruptly, "your socks don't match." A pang of rejection caused her gray eyes to flinch. At home later on she explained her story, once again seeking comfort. "Dear," the woman said sweetly "wear whatever makes you happy. Being different is OK."

Now the girl is not so little anymore. An adolescent she enters the eighth grade. As swirls of fashion labels and "popular" music permeate the school, she remained wearing what she feels comfortable in. Sitting attentively in English class, her teacher asked a simple question. "What is the most important thing to you?"

"GIRLS!" shouted a hormonally challenged boy. As the laughter died down, responses of friends, family, religion were heard throughout the classroom. The girl, feeling brave on that certain day, slowly raised her hand. "Yes, Emily," her teacher asked. "The most important thing to me is to be my own individual." Her teacher, hesitating for a second, had a look of surprise upon her face. "That's an excellent answer," she finally replied.

"Thanks," Emily said, "I learned that from my mother."

When You Finally Understand

I sat squirming madly on the hard wooden pew, vigorously running my fingers over the itchy tights that irritated my legs. The black shoes seemed to be squeezing my toes to the point where I was beginning to think I could never walk right ever again. At the age of five it was extremely difficult to concentrate on the priest in front monotonously droning on about something in which I was not interested or could not even comprehend for that matter. I constantly grabbed my brother's wrist trying to read his watch. The ticking seemed to pulsate throughout the silence of the mass, magnifying the sound one hundred times louder in my brain. All of a sudden everyone stood. Bewildered as to how everyone just knew when to sit, stand or kneel, I gathered up all my strength to actually put weight on my feet. Carefully putting my foot down and OUCH! I couldn't stand those shoes anymore — they had to go. Looking left at my mother, then right at my father, I slyly reached down and began to unbuckle my shoe. Finally free I stretched my toes out and wiggled them around. Now that my feet were taken care of, I longed to go home and take off the tights, the dress and to undo my hair. I just longed to be away from church. Finally, smiling as I recognized the closing prayer, I cheerfully followed my family out of the church and to the car. As some people around me felt a new "air" to their souls, I merely climbed into our car without a second thought as to what I had been doing the last hour.

"MO-OMM do I HAVE to go!" I whined with the extra annoying voice of a teenager. It was once again Tuesday night and time to go to CCD. CCD — the only thing worse than church. It was where I had to go and learn about church.

"I don't want to hear this from you again, Emily. You're going and that's final," my mother's voice had become stern. Her eyes looked at me with disapproval and I turned to look out my window to escape them. Pulling up to the church, I sat motionless for almost a whole minute before getting out. Closing the door a little harder than I should have, I walked towards my next hour of boredom. In class I sat cross-legged in the cheap plastic chairs that were a bit too small. While my eyes, my ears, and my presence remained open; my mind wandered far. I knew the stories they were preaching: Noah and his Ark, Adam and Eve, etc. I knew and respected the religious holidays. While a bible and rosary resided in my room, I did not pray outside of my own company. I knew the messages they were sending, the ideas that they were trying to plant into my head; many of which I did not agree with. I sat and listened about the evils of homosexuality and abortion. At the end of the hour I walked back outside happy only at the fact that I would not have to come back here for another whole week.

On Valentine's Day of last year, I was walking through the mall with three friends. While we passed stores filled with red and pink cards, I began to explain to them why I was late meeting them that day. "My parents actually made me go to church! I mean, it's not that I don't like God, but come on, Dad, I have a social life!"

I did not comprehend the morals that my parents were trying to instill in me. They knew that later on I would need religion to fall back on. However, I was focused on the mall. I complained on for a good fifteen minutes before I let it drop.

Later on, while we were eating dinner, I went to call my parents to tell them what time I would be arriving home. Dropping the quarter into the pay phone, I dialed and waited for someone at my house to pick up. Staring at the pink hearts and wondering why even the telephones were decorated, I was wondering why it was taking so long for someone to answer the phone. Since the answering machine was not picking up. I knew someone must be talking on the other line. Reaching into my pocket and pulling out yet another 25 cents, I once again dialed my number.

This time my Mom picked up on the first ring. "Mom, is it OK if I'm home by ten?" I asked.

"Emmie, I think it's better if you and your friends come home right after dinner and just stay here tonight." Puzzled as to why she would change plans when we had already discussed this in advance, I was about to protest when she explained herself. "Your father's at the nursing home, your Grandmother's . . . not doing so well." Understanding what she meant I told her to ask my brother to come and get us right away.

Returning to the restaurant, I told my friends to pay the check. We had only ordered drinks, so we threw a ten on the table, and went outside. Standing in the cold, I began to think about how sick my grandmother looked the last time I had seen her. She was very old and our family had been expecting this for some time now. Still, it was hard to think of someone who had been there all your life suddenly not be there anymore. I remembered staying at her house and having her show me her millions of old pictures. She would always be waiting with flat soda and chocolate covered-cherries. I was the youngest grandchild, so I was never around my grandmother as much as all the other kids, but I still loved her very much.

My friends, unknowing how I would handle this situation, asked me what they could do. "Hold my hand while I pray." Three pairs of eyes looked at me in total amazement. The only things they had heard about my religious life was how much I disliked church, CCD, etc. To their surprise, I took a deep breath and began to pray. The words came out of my mouth, slowly and quietly like they did at Mass. The only difference was that now a tone of sincerity and meaning came through. For the first time in my life, I had no one else to turn to than God.

Expressions

In the sixth grade, Mrs. Waggoner asked her class of 11-year-olds to do something they had never done before. Instructing everyone to take out a sheet of blank paper, she told the naive group to write down the exact emotions we were feeling at that time. Moans of displeasure were heard throughout the classroom in objection to the lesson. I, with pen in hand, scratched down one word. That one word led to two, two led to four. By the end of the half-hour, I had constructed my first poem. Some students breathed a sigh of relief as our disappointed teacher switched to a different lesson. No sound escaped my lips as I continued writing.

Now a sophomore in high school, I can't even contemplate a day without writing a least a fragment of a poem. Faced with hard days of classes in school and stressful nights of lots and lots of homework and the mix of emotions that teenagers are always faced with, I am always carrying pen and paper with me. Well-worn hardcover journals and notebooks line my bookshelf. Scraps of paper can be found on just about every piece of furniture of my room, as well as pens lying conveniently next to them.

After my grandmother died, after my brother and sister left home, after my nephew was born, I was found curled up in my room scrawling madly. While others let the whole world know how they feel, my soul finds its way up through my insides down to my fingers and finally onto paper. Some work is stained with tears; others can be barely read because my hand had to race to catch up to my thoughts.

Very few eyes have scanned over the words, lines and pages that I have written. While it provides a blanket from criticizing tongues, it also puts a leash on my creativeness. I would love to expand my ability, but my sensitivity gets the best of me. My poetry reflects who I am, who I want to be and the person inside longing to get out and express her ideas once in a while.

When Statues Cry

All my life I had never wanted anything more than to be just like my sister. Daina, who is seven years older than me, is my ultimate idol and a person I strive to be like.

From the time that I was born, I always had special feelings for my sister. Pictures of her holding me when I was a baby show me staring up at her, mesmerized by the energy that shone from her. At that age, I was her pet, her baby doll, and I adored the attention she gave me. An intangible bond formed at that very young age that will never be severed no matter how sharp a force tries to come between us.

As I became older and began to walk and talk, I would follow her around and mock the things she did or said. Many times I would sneak into her room, and dress up in her clothes. I would pull on her tattered jeans, which to me were "sooooo cool." Following would be a black T-shirt with the latest heavy metal band on the front. Finally I would carefully pick through the makeup scattered over the dresser and try (unsuccessfully) to recreate her look. Frosty pink lipstick smeared way above my lips and blue eye shadow traveled where it never had before. I looked like Madonna gone through the car wash, but I beamed from the inside thinking that I was just like my sister.

Slowly, I began to put her up on a mile-high pedestal that could not be reached. To me, she was God's greatest creation, perfect in every way and could never be equaled.

Unfortunately, she was not as affectionate towards me as I was towards her. Like all older sisters, she would get annoyed with a tag-along and frustrated with me. As she entered her teen years, she ran into problems with peer pressure and her grades began to drop. She developed a very negative attitude and an unpleasant aura loomed over her. To everyone else, she was a "troubled teen"; to me, she was a goddess who I would strive to be like. I was too young to understand the problems she was going through, all I saw was a beautiful person who was funny and had a very strong sense of who she was. At times she could be the most hilarious person to be around. She could turn any bad situation into a comic showcase. My personal favorite is when she would mock my dad. When he gets mad, he makes unusual faces and rolls his eyes. Daina, usually the one being yelled at, would stand behind him with her hand on her hips and mimic every little movement. Of course, she was exaggerating them to the point where it had my brother and me rolling on the floor. Her blonde hair, always done up, flying back and forth while she clicked her long press-on nails together. I watched every movement in envy, thinking she was so sure of herself that not even my dad affected her.

As I entered middle school, I started to suffer from a low self-esteem. I longed for the strength that my sister possessed and wondered why I could not be like her. I hated the way I looked to the point where I would get so frustrated with my appearance I would cry. I saw my sister, and how beautiful she was. I saw how she touched so many people. She was like the lights that draw gnats and flies; constantly glowing and buzzing with life. Nothing seemed to negatively affect her. She was like sculpture, beautiful and elegant, and untouchable. She seemed to stand above the rest — cool, calm and collected. Daina always seemed so sure of herself and independent. Everything I thought she possessed, I wanted. I beat myself up inside, tore into my soul to try to understand why I had to live in the shadow of her. All I could think about was how at my age, my sister was beautiful and popular and "cool." I ignored the report cards she brought home with F's and D's. I paid no attention to the cigarettes scattered across her room. I looked the other way when she yelled and fought with my mother, at times bringing the fragile woman to tears. I only saw the beauty that she possessed. Due to all this, I had become unsure of myself and very negative about my talents and my appearance.

About the middle of my seventh grade year, the pressure began to build. I was on the verge of childhood and adolescence, I was not happy with myself, and my sister and I had started to become very cruel to each other. I still envied her, and still loved her, but she was making my self-esteem worse. We would fight and bicker back and forth over petty things. I would say the cruelest things and she would relay the cruelty back to me, until one night neither of us could take it anymore. I saw my sister cry, really cry, for the first time. Not the tears of cutting your finger, or losing a boyfriend, but the tears of true pain and weakness. I saw my idol, my angel, my greatest symbol of strength, break down right in front of me.

We talked and talked for hours. I found out that a lot of her humor was a front that she put on to hide her true emotions. The pain inside her was equal to mine, she felt that she was not pretty enough, or good enough, for anyone. She confessed that while she laughed things off on the outside, inside they affected her deeply. Such as my father. During those years, my sister and father did not have the best relationship. I, thinking that it did not affect her, saw her pouring tears over her big green eyes of how she envied my relationship with my father.

Daina envies ME? The thought was too unbelievable to fully process at the time. She shared her insecurities, I shared my shoulder. She cried about her fears, I let go of mine. I crossed the line of maturity that night. I came to the realization that no one is perfect and that my sister did have problems of her own. I realized that no one should be put on a pedestal for no person is above another person. Most importantly, I realized that my sister and I are more alike than I ever thought we were. Even though I still envy her sometimes, and I still have a lowered self-esteem, I have accepted the fact that she and I both have our talents and flaws. That we were, and are, each special in our own way.

Unspoken Actions

One chilly morning I stepped out of my house into pitch-blackness that loomed over the town. I watched my breath swirl majestically around my face, dancing with the blunt coldness of the morning. Off in the distance I heard the wailing of an ambulance. Thinking it was only the fire station down the road, I put it out of my mind.

At the bus stop I gripped my jacket tightly around me to block out winter's cruel breath. The bus was unusually late this morning. Around me kids were coming and standing in their usual spots on the corner. Some lit cigarettes and the small red lights were the only evidence of people standing in the darkness. Becoming more irritated at the bus's failure to show, I turned and looked up the street. Finally, I saw the headlights creep around the corner and blind all the half-awake teenagers who slowly began to gather their backpacks and climb up in the bus. Forcing my tired legs up the steps I began to search for my best friend, Jenni. Making my way almost to the back, I still did not see her. Sitting in the first unoccupied seat I saw, I wondered what could have possibly happened between the time I called her that morning and the time I reached the bus. Knowing she wasn't sick, I remembered the ambulance I had heard. A sick feeling griped my stomach as I began to overhear a conversation of the two girls in front of me. "She FLIPPED over the car!! Or at least that's what that guy was saying. If I had come out of my house like two minutes earlier I would have seen the whole thing. There was BLOOD on the road and glass everywhere!"

I knew. I didn't need anymore explanation, in my heart I knew that she was talking about Jenni. I worried every morning about her crossing that road. It was a very busy, very dangerous intersection with no crosswalk. I began to piece everything together. "Flipped over the car" — the ambulance sirens — her missed presence on the bus. All the way to school I fought back the tears that stung my eyelids.

As the bus pulled to the front of the school, I walked right in the door to the pay phones. Ignoring everyone around me, I fished 35 cents out of my pocket. "Mom! Jenni has been hit by a car." I said the words more calmly than I would have ever expected. My mother reassured me that she and my sister would be there as soon as possible. Ignoring the warning bell for first period I went and stood outside. Sitting on the bench letting the wind blow through my hair, I sat and thought about when Jenni and I first met . . .

I walked into the overcrowded room of buzzing adolescents. Not recognizing one single face, I saw a girl sitting alone. She wore the same jeans as me and she seemed to be looking for familiar faces too. I took a chance and walked over to her.

"Hi, I'm Emily, can I sit here?"

I held my breath as I waited for an answer. Knowing how cruel children can be, I half expected a harsh "NO". Luckily she only smiled warmly.

"Sure you can sit here," she replied, "My name is Jenni."

For the next hour of orientation we sat and laughed at all our new teachers. We exchanged phone numbers. We even examined each other's schedules and saw that we had four classes together. As we got up to go home, Jenni grabbed my hand and squeezed it. I looked down bewildered at the gesture.

"Why did you do that?" I asked.

Jenni turned and smiled, "Because you being with me helped me get through this. I was really nervous about all of this."

My lips formed a smile as I squeezed her hand back . . .

My mom and sister pulled up quickly. I got up and practically ran to the car. Throwing open the door and tossing in my backpack I jumped in. My sister was driving; my mother had sheer worry in her eyes. "Do you know what hospital she's in?" I asked. Daina merely nodded her head. The gray morning looked ominous as we completed the drive to the hospital in silence.

Walking into the hospital I instantly spotted Jenni's grandparents. Her Grandmother's frail frame looked weak and her eyes were red and swollen. Exchanging hugs, I then noticed the tears in her Grandfather's eyes. Taking a seat in the waiting room, I was reluctant to ask any questions. The hospital smelled like a new car to me. The chairs were almost as uncomfortable as the atmosphere. The walls and floors seemed to not meet at a fixed place, just molded into each other.

Everything was white, making me think of heaven. I pushed any thought of death out of my mind as finally Jenni's grandparents explained the details to me.

Jenni had been crossing the street to walk to the bus stop when a woman driving to work struck her. She had fractured her pelvis, shattered her leg and her arm had completely rotated in a full circle. Her leg bone was going to be put back together and held in place by a metal rod. Her arm was going to need corrective surgery and pins were needed to keep it in place while healing. At that point in time, no one knew about internal damage.

As I was being told all of this my jaw felt like it had hit the shiny floor. I did not know whether to cry or just to be thankful that she was alive. I pushed my hair out of my face and took a deep breath. Feeling the stinging behind my eyelids, I was relieved to see that the nurse had come over to talk to us.

"You can come and see her now," she said blankly. No emotion, no sympathy. Her voice and face lacked what the whole hospital lacked — color.

Walking up to Jenni's room, I began to try and gather myself, but nothing could prepare me for the sight that I was about to see. I turned the corner and saw her lying on the bed. Her broken body looked awkward. Machines surrounded her on every side. Tubes were coming out of her mouth and nose. Splints on her arm and leg showed signs of blood seeping through. There were traces of glass, dirt and blood on her face that was scratched and bruised. Her skin was yet another thing that lacked any color and her eyes were closed tightly. An eerie silence was suffocating the room. I wanted to talk to her; I wanted to shout at her. I wanted to let her know just how much I loved her. I wanted her to be the one standing up, breathing perfectly. With her mom, her grandparents, my mother, and my sister watching me, I could only stand there and let the tears overflow dripping onto the floor.

I saw her hand, her right hand lying softly on the bed. It seemed to be the only part of her body that looked normal and healthy. I reached down and squeezed her palm gently. After a whole minute, the flow of tears increased as nothing was felt in response. I squeezed again, my hand gripping harder now. Tears streaming like a waterfall, I looked hopelessly at Jenni. Please, please just open your eyes for one second. My body feeling the beginning of powerful sobs threatening to overcome me, I felt something twitch in my hand.

I stopped crying and looked down. Could it be? Once again she had gathered up whatever strength she possessed and Jenni squeezed my hand.

Winter of the Spring

The room feels like winter. Snow-white walls meet white floors meet her bed. Her struggle for air in and out — in and out — hits the surface like angry December wind and dies among the shadows. Her body, static in the middle of the room, looks like snow angels I made as a child. Nothing was firm, everything moldable in those days. But now electric robots stand looking down with long unfamiliar arms that invade her body and rob her of normalcy.

As my mind escapes the boundaries of the room, I remember the days of warmth. Me as a little child, in her arms — dancing. Pockets full of posies that fell onto the sun-kissed earth. Picnics with the lily's gaze upon us, she would make peanut butter and jelly sandwiches with the crusts cut off. Her, lying next to me singing Amazing Grace while I explained what the clouds looked like that day. We would lie like that until dusk began to force the sun away. Then night would claim my fantasy and she would tuck me in with a song. Smile once, kiss me twice, and —

SLAM! I am snapped back into the present with an abrupt shutting of the door. Strangers with white coats travel in and out and I do not understand why they try and brave this blizzard. They wax philosophical while adjusting the robot faces. I want to tell them, "Stay at home, please, with your children and spouses and siblings. Be their blanket in this world. Leave us here to freeze together." For here only empty chairs, hard and wooden, stand staring in her direction. I sit below, on the floor, feeling cold, cold, cold.

Shades are drawn and enclose us in our prison from the evil sun and evil world of healthy happy people. I make pretend snowballs with my fingers as I stare, up onto the bed, at my snow angel. She was once a sauna for my love, but now is when I'm cold. Now is when I freeze.

The steady rise and fall of her chest stutters, as her wind becomes unrhythmic. I stand to investigate, and see the cancer on her face. Her once peaceful disposition is disrupted. Her cheek flinches and mouth contorts in tiny bites of pain. The mouth that once had sung to me on dreamy days of youth was now mute. I start to choke on the horrible feeling that has crept up from my stomach. I want to dance in the backyard again. "Hold me," I want to say, "Clothe me from the cold. I can make peanut butter and jelly sandwiches if you will just let us walk away from here." If she would only open her eyes, her knowing gaze would calm me down. But then again, if her eyes were open I could see the infestation in her soul. I swallow deeply as she exhales, and now I feel it in her breath. It's freezing her from the inside out and attacking at me and the room. I yell internally and pray for its retreat.

Once more the pattern of her breathing becomes unbroken. The white-coated strangers breeze back into our winter. They surround her like little children building angels in the snow, but she is already complete — her fate undeniably built. Minutes chase eternity in vain. An announcement of the time cuts through the thinning air, as they file one by one back out into the world to leave me here and shiver. Two tears roll down, kissing either cheek, as I watch my snow angel fade away from the bed. This masterpiece that should have lasted so much longer than this winter is melting with the dawn of spring. Turning away, I walk over to the window and lift the shades. I tell the walls what the clouds look like, and stare back at a lily in the garden.

And this was the day I lost my mother.

The First Day

The first day in a new place never bothered me. I was eight the last time I moved. I adored attention and I thrived on people watching me perform, talk, sing, anything. So when I moved here to Centreville, I was extremely excited for my first day of school.

The school was not nearly as big as my other one so I wasn't intimidated by the building. When I walked into my classroom, I saw my new teacher had a kind face and smile. The very first thing she did was have me tell the class about myself and about where I used to live. It was like being on stage! I loved it. I talked and talked. I think she had to make me stop talking. My mind was racing and I couldn't wait to get to know everyone.

As I sat at my desk, I began chatting with some people; luckily, everyone was kind. I felt so warm and welcomed that I was totally open and comfortable. The kids here were no different from my friends in California. They all watched the same TV shows, listened to the same music, played the same games. I thought back to my friends in California at one point. Did they miss me? Did they just continue on the same without me? They probably were, it's just a fact of life that people come and go. There is nothing I could do to stop it. The people I met that day would be there every day for the rest of the year. I would talk and interact and learn from them, but would it make a difference if one of them left, or if I left.

The events of each day would continue on without fail.

At the end of the day, I was almost sad to go home. I hadn't gotten enough time to talk to everyone and I really wanted to talk more. On the bus ride home, I thought about the events of the day and I was happy with myself that I was such an open person and I really liked it here. Overall, my experience was definitely a good one.

Barbie Story

She somehow couldn't get the feeling back. She stroked Barbie's glistening plastic back with the tip of her index finger attempting to conjure the revelation about life she had experienced ecstatically just moments before. Barbie's tiny purple sweatsuit lay strewn on the floor in a fit of her maddening lust and now she stood naked, clasped in the girl's fist and heaving, because as the commercial's disclaimer proclaims, "Barbie cannot stand alone." Ken also sat in the corner. His head would later melt in the girl's Easy-Bake Oven, which she rather ingeniously powered by alternate current from her father's car battery. He drove a used Escort. The bulb in the miniature oven exploded instantly from the excess charge and nicked her ring-fingernail so that it made an interesting arc of split quick. Ken's melted head began to cascade in syrupy ropes into the little tray at the bottom and Barbie suddenly appeared to jump up and down in glee from her standing position, propped up against the brick wall of the garage and still sans sweatshirt.

"Finally!" exclaimed Barbie, and suddenly regretted the spontaneous outburst that had escaped her. Suddenly, the girl turned abruptly, ending Ken's ritualistic execution. He stood stuck to the floor, a classical body figure absent a head. Barbie tried to return her mouth to the tight pink-lipped smile it was before, but failed and started to distort her mouth in several different positions to relax the muscles that, prior to her shouting, had been non-existent. The girl shook her head, blinked twice, and slumped down onto the concrete. She placed her hand, by accident, in the pool of plastic liquid that was formerly Ken's head.

"Well, is it so hard to believe that I have a voice?" demanded the four and one-third inch woman that now stood before the gawking girl. As Barbie walked from the wall, the girl saw her breasts shrink considerably and her stomach become more curvaceous. Barbie's firm skin also became somewhat looser, and her bright blue eyes dulled to a light but distinct gray.

"No, but I thought the only thing you ever said was, 'Let's take a ride in my brand new car,' and 'Let's throw a party!'"

"No, that's only what you heard. I say lots of things."

"Oh," the little girl looked off with a disappointed stare. In confusion, tears started pooling in her innocent eyes and began falling slowly to the floor. Barbie's now living face showed a distraught expression. She had never meant to hurt the little girl's feelings, but she was annoyed with the trembling lip.

"Oh, I'm sorry, it's just, well, I've been stuck with these stupid pointed feet and this bleach blond hair for years. Now I just . . ." Barbie's voice trailed off.

"Ken's dead," the girl whispered guiltily.

"As is obvious by the remains of his head that are stuck to the inside of your oven . . . You know, I think I like being naked."

The girl looked again at Barbie's now very anatomically correct body and shyly looked away.

"This is great!" Barbie shouted, doing a handstand and dodging the flab of glossy flesh that almost struck her in the chin. Her breasts seemed less "perky" than before.

"I have some of Ken's clothes in my room if you want to get changed or something," the girl murmured, disassembling Ken's elaborate torture chamber and scraping off the mess in the oven with her fingernail.

"Who doesn't?" Barbie sneered. "That bastard's been all around the toy box. I've seen him necking with Midge, smooching his plastic smile all over her freckly face."

The girl blushed. Yes, she had made Ken do that before.

"And I'm not 'Barbie' anymore . . . call me . . . what's a good solid name? I need a fierce, naked, bleached blonde name that Ken will shout all the way to his portion of hell."

The girl didn't answer, just scraped, and contemplated the stench arising from her little oven and what she should do with this living doll that demanded a naked name.

"Jane," the doll said triumphantly, looking up at the girl. "My name will be Jane."

And so, for the next few weeks Jane continued to live, naked and voluptuous, inside the girl's room. At first she walked back and forth across the dressing table, moving ribbons and throwing all her tiny Barbie accessories away. She admired herself in the mirror as she worked, throwing away the garbage of this pink constraint in which she had previously existed. Her muscles would flex and retract and soon all the toys began to stare. Naked dolls were no strangers to their community, but Jane had brought something different.

The girl, too, felt the difference in her room. She began to fear going in, began to fear the continuous stream of propaganda that spouted from Jane's mouth. She came home late from school and left early. She entered dance classes that her mother had always tried to enroll her in. She did everything she could to stay away from her room that was tainted by the strange naked woman. Jane, as she liked to call herself, became more and more of a problem. Sometimes the girl would come home to find her entire room in disarray, and then she would simply look at Jane and let out a depressive sigh. The sight of the now bloated "Barbie" made her sick to her stomach and she definitely needed to do something to fix it. Jane had to go.

"Oh no, dear . . . oh no no no no!" Jane gleefully chirped. "You're not getting rid of me anytime soon." The girl gasped and brought her hands to her face. So she could read thoughts now?! To what limits would this strange creature strive?

Jane lounged on the dresser, flopping about and stretching. Jane Fonda's workout tape was in the VCR but Jane didn't really seem to be following, merely mocking it and moving to her own rhythm.

"Why are you so many strange women, to so many strange people, you strange girl?" Jane purred and kicked her legs in the air. They had once been long and shapely and now, were short and showed little bumps of stubble. "This is a part of you. I am you. You have no name. I have one. My name is Jane."

She proceeded to jump to her feet and unscrew the lid from the girl's large jar of perfumed cream, with some effort, due to the fact that it was larger than she was. She scooped up the white cold cream with tiny hands and smeared it into a word on the girl's mirror, which was adorned with childish stickers and pictures of giggling friends. The word was FAITH. The girl looked at the mirror and suddenly saw herself as if for the first time. She stood in her leotard and saw the small curve of her small body around her abdomen. Despite dance classes, her body still possessed a thin layer of softness.

"I've missed you, chica," Barbie laughed, smacking her hands together and dripping cream on herself and the surface of the dresser. "You've been away for too long and I've had to take care of Midge. Midge was your favorite, wasn't she?"

"No, you were." Midge walked out of the "Barbie Mansion," which was hollow, cheaply adorned with sticker art, and occupied by broken, dog-chewed stairs. Instead of her long crimped hair, a short bob grazed her shoulders. Her bikini, that changed colors in the cold water, seemed about to break and her hard plastic body began to soften and move as she walked.

"Am I still your favorite now?" Midge asked as her formerly stiff lips twisted into a coy smile. Jane laughed and the two embraced each other and then looked expectantly at the girl. The four eyes stared directly and purposefully at the girl. Something inside her eight-year-old mind broke and she began to cry. Salty lines ran down her face and over a newfound smile. For the first time in her short life, the girl saw profound beauty in the two small dolls and in her own reflection beyond them. Jane broke a smile too. Her grip tightened around Midge's waist and her eyes darted in the direction of her plastic house.

"You know, handicapped Barbie's wheelchair can't fit through that door," Jane said as her slack mouth jumped a little at the corners.

The girl started to laugh slightly. "I have a curling iron in my bathroom," she said as she wiped her face with her small open palms. "It might take a while."

"Time's what we got," Midge chirped, and it reminded the girl of a television show her parents had forbidden her to watch. It was about a jailbreak — a handsome inmate dressed in a gray uniform had said the exact same thing as he chipped away at the wall of his cell with a spoon.

They set to work. The doorway itself didn't take nearly as long as the rest of the tiny house, which they melted with the enthusiastic ecstasy that arises from unplanned adventures. After the house became a vertical mass of lava that began to adhere to the white carpet, the girl asked the two dolls, "What now?"

They did not speak. Barbie and Midge just lay plastic, lifeless and glossy on the floor, their mouths frozen and tinted. The girl gathered them and all of the dolls around her room. One by one she melted them until a mountain of plastic had fully bonded with the floor, vibrant with swirls of pink and purple. Her room now void of color, white and simple, seemed to be comfortable and new again. She stood and walked to her desk. Fishing out a paper scrap and her father's old ballpoint pen, she wrote her name and stuck the scrap on the mirror where the cold cream had dried. Looking at herself, smiling, the paper staring at her read "FAITH."

Cortney Kreer contributed to the writing of this story.

Genesis Relived

You are going to be told you a story that is, in its entirety, completely and utterly true. Now, many may try to deny its validity, but those who refuse to believe are only shutting off their minds to their faith. Not everything in this world is a consequence or a reaction to a specific act of science. Some occurrences are God's acts and God's acts alone. So with this out of the way, listen intently to this tale.

Isabelle was a woman with no past and in all likelihood, no future either. She lived alone, it had seemed, forever. Though someone must have bore this woman, she possessed no recollection of any maternal figure. Her memory only held the isolated childhood and now adulthood in which she lived. Of course, this might be impossible for some to believe. How could someone live completely alone right from birth and survive? How did she feed herself before she could walk? How did she learn to walk for that matter? The answer is one that has no evidence, just needs the simple trust of the reader. Isabelle grew from infant to woman with no external factors other than the woods in which she lived. She lived her life by the cycle of night and day, sun and moon, and years only showed when she aged.

It was on one rather chilly day that her life was altered. Something she had never seen before walked up the road towards her cabin. After it approached and knocked, twice abruptly, on the door she saw that it was a man. He asked politely if he could come in, that he was tired and hungry and would appreciate a place to rest. She opened the door but informed him that she unfortunately had only one bed. He told her that it was not necessary and rather improper for him to take her bed and that he would gladly sleep on the floor by the fire. Isabelle, shaken at the new presence in her home, said it was all right but slept half-awake for she felt the man was not to be trusted.

In the morning, the man rose long after sunrise to find Isabelle already outside washing the few garments of clothing and blankets that she had. He stood at the doorway and watched her. The sun caught the highlights in her long hair that was curled naturally on the ends. As her arms worked her muscles extended and retracted like machinery, only elegant and bronzed to something beautiful. The man knew that this was what he had set out to find.

Isabelle felt eyes on her and turned, wet from water and sweat, to see the stranger staring at her. Though she never knew a man before, never felt a man's eyes before, she still felt that it was wrong for this man to glare at her body like some sort of animal getting ready to pounce on dinner. She had watched the mountain lions long enough to know the look. She asked him shortly if he would like some breakfast before he was to be on his way. He said that he wasn't leaving because his ankle had swelled over the night and he could barely walk. She looked down and saw that, indeed, his left ankle was purple and round.

Isabelle walked from the water and tore a piece of cloth off a blanket hanging from a tree. She asked the man to sit down, and then began to bind the ankle as if she had dressed a thousand wounds before. The man asked her name. She told him that she called herself Isabelle. He inquired whether anyone else called her that. She answered she had never known anyone and therefore named herself. He asked of her mother, she in turn asked what a mother was. The man looked at her strangely and then coyly smiled. Yes, this is who he had been looking for. Isabelle asked the stranger's name in return. He told her that his name was Lucius.

For the next few weeks the man's ankle remained purple and round. Daily the two would follow the same routine, and at night they had become accustomed to talking. Lucius told Isabelle of the places he had walked and traveled and the things that he had seen. Isabelle described her life of solitude. Through these nightly interactions Isabelle had found herself attracted to her visitor, something that she had never felt before. His dark hair was black like the soil at night and fell into his eyes when he laughed. Deep lines on his face proved that he had weathered many towns and villages and years. His eyes were pure blue like the river water when the sun was at its hottest time of year. Despite all of this, something told her that her feelings were wrong. Though she was drawn to Lucius, she knew she must try to resist him, but a reason for this was nonexistent.

Finally, Lucius's ankle returned to its normal state and he again walked with confidence and purpose. He told Isabelle that he would leave if she wished him to. Though a thousand voices inside her screamed to let him leave, she answered no and that she would like him to stay with her. Lucius smiled, almost proudly, and he walked towards her. That night, Lucius did not sleep on the floor by the fire.

When Isabelle awoke, she found her bed distorted. The once glowing oak with white simple sheets was now old and decaying. Her long hair was gone in patches, and her eyes burned. Her quaint cabin in the woods was charred and a slight draft chilled her body. Isabelle screamed for Lucius, and he came to her smiling. She demanded to know what had happened. Lucius asked her if she had ever read the bible. Isabelle again screamed no and asked what he had done to her house. Lucius then explained to her what she had done. Isabelle collapsed and wept.

Now, though that is the end of the story, it is quite certain that the reader needs some explanations. Isabelle's real name had been Eve. She had a partner, Adam, who had died when they were both young. Isabelle lived on the mountain of Eden, and now the story is most certainly quite familiar. What is not clear, however, is that this story is the story of the beginning of the second world — our world. God had cleared his first experiment with man when Lucifer had finally gotten control of 90 — yes 90 — percent of the population. So in two easy acts, God erased the world, sending those 90 percent to rest with Lucifer. Hoping that those millions of people would be satisfaction enough, God recreated his world as explained in Genesis. The bible was left untouched, seeing as how if rewritten it would show that Lucifer had won over God at one time. In the unwritten story Eden was not a garden, but a mountain. Adam and Eve were born, through God, as babies. Adam, however, could not survive in the new environment. Eve grew beautifully. Though the experiment was going well, Lucifer caught wind of God's plan and, never able to be content, embarked on a journey to again tempt Eve as he did before. Knowing the serpent disguise was overdone, Lucifer came as something he knew Eve could not resist — a man.

From this, of course, comes original sin, the expulsion from paradise, etc. However, in this story the serpent is not the villain, the villain is man. And so, what the reader learns from this is solely his or her own interpretation. However, it is certain that the reader will never look at a man in the same way.

Log #4

I felt at one with the universe in a great time of pain. A car had hit my best friend and I had seen her lying in a hospital bed. I went home and tried to sleep but I could not get the image out of my head. Her face was pale and bloody and she was struggling to breathe. Hooked up to machines, she even couldn't breathe or eat on her own.

That night I got up from my bed and walked out onto my back porch. It was a chilly September evening and the wind was blowing. I sat on the wooden railing and got lost inside the wind. I don't even remember what I was looking at; I just remember the wind seemed to blow right through me, down to my soul. Nothing else seemed to be around. My thoughts were the only things that consumed me and for the first time all day I wasn't crying. An eerie sense of calm and aloneness were with me as I sat there. The houses, the trees, my dog, they all disappeared and only the wind and sky were left.

I thought about everything, but I didn't analyze anything. I just remembered everything that Jenni and I had been through and how much I loved her and how I couldn't think what life would be like without her. I thought about how I wished it were me who was hit by the car, not her. I wished I could take away all her pain and give her the feeling of calm that I had right now. The blackness of the sky seemed to match my mood and I stared into the stars for answers. The wind seemed to have lifted my soul to a higher level and I was deeper inside myself than I had ever seen before.

I don't know how long I was out there, or exactly what made me slip into a state like that, but I know it was an odd experience. Things happen in life, and now I know that I can't explain them or change them. Life has a way of making things happen for a reason and I had to accept that. I think that night was a way of letting myself know that I couldn't handle everything alone, but I had to stop and gain control of my own sanity before I could help others and let others help me.

Hockey Sticks and Cigarettes

He came 30 minutes early. His eyes were swollen from the lack of sleep and he was craving a real meal. The artificial hospital food he had been living on was attacking his insides. He sat quietly gazing out the window. It was hazy out; it looked as if it would start to rain soon. How did he get here? It was ridiculous — Saturday morning detention for what they thought was skipping, but he had to. It was skipping in a way. He had to make a last-minute decision. He had to leave. The school would have never accepted his note anyway. He knew what they thought of him. He was well aware of his reputation.

He was a pariah in his school, and he liked it like that. All the flaunting of your riches, being in a certain clique, it was all futile to him. Everyone was scared of him. They talked about his wardrobe, which consisted of only three shirts, a pair of black combat boots, and two pairs of cargo pants he wore continually. There were rumors of what he did after school. He didn't mind them. He was promethean in his own way. He didn't want to be like them. In walked Mr. Parker . . .

"Why are you early?" Earl Parker's stern voice jerked Blane Howard out of his daydream. "I'm here for the Saturday detention — that you gave me," Blane said coldly.

Mr. Parker paused momentarily, disgustedly looking into Blane's eyes. They were like two pieces of coal. Blane's dirty brown hair, long and uncared for, framed his pale face. A black shirt with an occasional hole covered his upper torso, which was well defined for a boy of his age. His baggy pants sagged below his waist and covered the scuffed black combat boots, leaving worn thread tailing his feet. A thick silver chain, a source of many rumors about Blane, led from his back pocket to his belt loop. Teenage gossip reported that he had beaten, strangled, or even killed a man with that chain. Mr. Parker's hatred for Blane increased by the second.

"Since you are here early anyway, you might as well start your time," Parker snickered. "I need you to take these 20 desks from this floor to room 322."

Blane knew that classroom was located on the very end of the last hallway on the third floor. With a tired body, Blane walked over and picked up the first desk. Climbing the stairs in the hollow hallways, with each step his foot came down hard like a block of cement. Mr. Parker walked away satisfied as Blane continued up the stairs with the desk clumsily being pulled along.

A half hour had passed and Blane was picking up the eighth desk when he suddenly heard footsteps behind him. Turning around he saw Thomas Anderson — better known as Tommy. Tommy was starting quarterback and valedictorian. His blonde hair was perfectly cut around his face. Two blue eyes set perfectly between a perfect nose and perfect smile.

"Are you here for detention too?" asked Tommy. Blane slightly nodded his head in response to the question and continued with his work. Tommy, always the cynosure of everything, impatiently continued.

"Hey, what are we supposed to do?"

Curtly Blane replied, "Desks, room 322."

Tommy, a little annoyed by Blane's bluntness, looked at the group of desks next to him. Shrugging, he grabbed one end of a desk and began to carelessly drag it along, following Blane's path. Every so often he would stop to check his reflection in the windows.

While fixing the part in his hair, Tommy felt a sharp pain as his knee hit a desk. Dropping the desk and grabbing his knee, he saw Blane crouched down on the floor tying his shoe. As he opened his mouth to yell, Mr. Parker's voice was heard from down the hall.

"HOWARD! Why have you stopped? Get back to work!"

Blane peered through the strands of hair covering his eyes. "I was only tying my shoe."

"I don't need to hear your excuses; I want those desks up there now!"

Blane swallowed the comment about to escape his tongue and resumed carrying the desk. Tommy on the other hand, decided to sit down and give his leg some time to rest.

"Didn't hurt ya too bad, did it?" Mr. Parker's tone was one of a sympathetic father. He stood over Tommy, thinking how ridiculous it was that this boy had detention on the day of the big game. He needed rest.

"I'll be OK," Tommy replied. Hoping that Mr. Parker would go back to his office, Tommy remained seated on the ground.

"You know, you really should be getting as much rest as possible for the game tonight. It's a big one ya' know. They're undefeated," Mr. Parker began to ramble on with statistics and words of encouragement.

Finally Tommy decided he would rather carry a desk up three flights of stairs than listen to his principal give him the same talk he heard every day before a game. He got up off the floor, took hold of the edge of the desk, and began to make his way upstairs.

Blane made his way back down the stairs and into the classroom. He looked relieved as he saw one final desk sitting in the corner. Tommy, nowhere to be seen, had done his share of carrying three whole desks. Blane grabbed the desk and began to trudge back up to the third floor for the last time. When he had approached the second floor, he saw Tommy sitting on the staircase.

Pulling a cigarette out of his pocket, he looked at Blane, "You got a light?" First looking over his shoulder, half expecting Mr. Parker to come walking around the corner, Blane finally replied, "No."

"Really? Wow, thought all guys like you always carried a pack."

"Actually I don't smoke," Blane looked down at Tommy. His pants were ironed and his shirt matched them perfectly. In fact, everything from head to toe was matching. Even the $100 shoes that covered his feet.

"Could've fooled me. What are you here for anyway — you kill someone else?" Tommy's lips curled in a tiny sneer as he inhaled his cigarette. Tossing his pack to the side, he stood up and directly faced Blane.

"Skipping. I was caught skipping," Blane chose to ignore the remark. Though he was about two inches taller, and had about 30 pounds more muscle, he didn't seem to intimidate Tommy at all.

"Me too. A bunch of old friends of mine were down from college for spring break. I decided to take my own spring break and join 'em. We got so trashed; it was worth a Saturday detention. What did you skip for?"

"My mom. She's sick in the hospital. Cancer." Tommy's eyes closed momentarily. Already regretting the rude comment he had made, he thought back to years ago. He remembered holding his father's hand while his mother lay pale in the hospital bed.

"I'm sorry," he said blankly.

"Why? What would you know about it?" Blane interjected.

Tommy took on a tone that was more serious than Blane had ever heard or expected out of his mouth. "My mother died of leukemia when I was ten."

Blane, shocked, took a place next to Tommy on the steps. They sat in silence on the steps for a long minute. With no words, they stood up and began to drag the desk upstairs side by side, each one holding one end.

Back down in the main hallway, Tommy and Blane began to leave. Each looking forward to their own days finally away from the school, when suddenly Mr. Parker's hounding voice was heard from the staircase.

"BOYS!"

Turning around, the boys saw Mr. Parker, rigid from anger and holding Tommy's pack of cigarettes. The principal looked at both of the boys. While he could never remember ever seeing Blane Howard with a cigarette, they certainly couldn't be Tommy's — could they?

"I suggest that one of you speak up for this," Mr. Parker said, though he was looking directly at Blane. His eyes piercing right through his innocent face. "Tommy, I know you would be smart enough not to smoke with your athletic ability." Mr. Parker's eyes never wavered off Blane. Tommy stood silent, knowing that if he spoke up he could lose his place on the team. He could lose his scholarship if he lost his place on the team. Blane looked at Tommy, looked at Mr. Parker, and then at the pack of cigarettes.

"They're mine," he said strongly.

An almost silent gasp of air escaped Tommy's lips in relief. Not silent enough, though.

Mr. Parker broke his gaze from Blane and looked directly into Tommy's eyes. Staring back at one another, Mr. Parker caught a slight glimpse of fear. The three stood looking at one another.

Mr. Parker altered his eyes from Tommy to Blane and back to Tommy.

"I'll deal with you on Monday." Mr. Parker said quietly to Blane. Turning he walked away and closed the door to his office.

"Thanks, man," Tommy said to Blane. Blane said nothing, only stared right past him. The coldness that was lost for only a short time was now again felt in Blane's presence. They walked out of the building together, through the doors into the rain that began to pour down from the gray clouds.

"TOMMY!" A group of students called from the far parking lot. Tommy looked first at Blane then turned and started to jog toward his friends.

Blane, pushing the hair out of his eyes, turned the opposite way and began to walk toward his car alone.

Xylophone

I wanted to play the xylophone. It was the most coveted instrument of the third grade. Every Tuesday morning Mrs. Patterson would assign wooden sticks, tambourines, bells, and recorders to our class. From the remaining ten, she would pick five of us to play the xylophone and five of us to sing. With five available positions a week, and about 24 kids in the class, everyone should have gotten a turn about once a month. Most of my girlfriends however, only played the xylophone once that year. In the nine long months of my third grade year, I was the only girl who played the xylophone about six times.

Looking at my family, one would think that I have traditional views of what a man and women should be. My mother is a housewife who does all the cooking, cleaning and nurturing while my father is the breadwinner and does yard work and fixes appliances. On the outside, they are a model couple for the domestic and public spheres. Their personal characteristics, however, are very different. My mother is outspoken, strong and determined. My father is sensitive, modest, and peaceful. My parents have strongly raised me and my siblings to believe that to be a healthy person, we should contain both feminine and masculine qualities.

In elementary school, I noticed many similarities and differences between my girlfriends and me. While like them I was in dance class and liked to play jump rose at recess, I was also on basketball and softball teams and sometimes played kickball with the boys. In class, I would always raise my hand, and speak out, and received much attention from my teachers.

When I asked my friend Amber why she didn't call out her answers even though she had the right ones, she told me, "Father told me it's not polite to speak out of turn." This was foreign to me. My mother had always said over and over that if you have something to say, say it. So I, in turn, did. I was never punished or reprimanded by my teachers; in fact, I was more positively reinforced with praise. At the same time I was never thought of as a tomboy by or ostracized from my girlfriends.

I was, however, horribly teased and ridiculed by the boys in my class. Without knowing it, I had defied the traditional definition of what a little "girl" should be. I was dominant in the classroom and tried to enter their "realm" on the playground. I had threatened them and their traditional privilege as males.

In high school, though I was not teased or the subject of ridicule by all boys, I still clearly made some of my classmates uncomfortable and even became the target of angst from some girls. When I debated with a guy in class, I was often called a "bitch" by him outside of class. In my own group of friends, mixed males and females, I often heard from my guy friends, "Wow, Emily, you're so awesome, you're just like one of the guys," because I could relate to them on many levels that my sensitive and passive female friends could not. My upbringing and understanding of what a "female" should act like was challenging the traditional view that most of my school had. I was a threat to many people because I challenged certain gender boundaries.

From the time I was born I have always been astutely aware that I was female, because the meaning of "female" is different to me than it is to many. Even though my generation was born and raised in a time when society acknowledged women's rights, we have been influenced that being female is being weak and submissive. Webster's dictionary even defines feminine as "having the qualities of a woman; becoming or appropriate to the female sex; as, in a good sense, modest, graceful, affectionate, and confiding; or, in a bad sense, weak, nerveless, timed, pleasure-loving, and effeminate." I was raised to believe that being female meant being strong, ambitious, and forceful with my ideas, as well as compassionate and sympathetic. Being female was playing basketball and performing in a dance recital. Because of this, I got many advantages that others did not, such as playing the more coveted instrument in third grade, or receiving more attention from teachers. I also got more ridicule for stepping out of my "place." Some can argue that I am more masculine than feminine, but I believe that I am a strong balance of the two.

Log #5

This log is difficult for me because I did not know my grandparents. I have no idea about my ancestors or their personality traits or their occupations, etc. So I thought that I would be unable to do this log. But, I thought I could do the log on just two of my ancestors.

My grandmother died a year before I was born. My middle name, Marjorie, is hers. My mom says that I remind her so much of my grandmother. First of all, I have her hair; no one else in my family has thick blond hair except for my aunt. Secondly, my mom says that I sound more and more like her the older I get. Nanny also had a passion for music, as do I. Another weird little thing is a habit that both she and I have. I press my knuckle to my cheek and bit the inside of my mouth. Now, that is not a common thing like biting your nails, so when my mom saw me do that when I was little she freaked out! That is something our family jokes about all the time. My mom also says that my spirit is just like my grandmother. She says that I try to get the most life out of life that I can, and that I am such a happy and giving person. I am proud to be like my grandmother. Even though I never knew her, everyone said that she was easy to love and a joy to be around.

My grandfather also died before I was born. He is my paternal grandfather, and I know more about him from my father. The personality trait that he, my dad and myself all share is that we all are extremely headstrong. My grandfather worked for the Justice Department and my dad works for the SEC and I would like to go into criminal investigation. My mother says that there is a certain "karma" about us that is different from everyone else. Another common thing that runs through this side of the family is that we are all strong, religious Catholics.

The symbol for my ancestors would have to be a cross, because of my paternal side's strong Catholic faith. My mother's side, while they were devout Lutherans, had a stronger spiritual connection with God. They didn't always go to church, but they were very goodhearted and faithful people.

Rant

I used to wonder why it was so hard for me to write. Now, I don't wonder, I just know what causes my impotence for writing standard five-paragraph thesis essays. The fact that they're standard. I mean, all during school, people tell us to be different, inventive, and creative. And then they crash all our ambitions and make us write boring essays on subjects we give two shits about. It screws with my ethics and makes me lose faith in the education that we are taught to value so much.

Another reason I know it is hard for me to write is because most of the subjects I am not very opinionated on, and for the most effective thesis paper, it's usually good to have an opinion you are trying to prove. Me, I personally don't care if Romeo and Juliet killed themselves out of love or typical teenage rebellion laced with raging hormones. In any event, they were both spoiled brats and the only death I was crying over was Mercutio. "So write about that!" I was told. And I did. And I still got a bad grade for my unenthusiastic prose, because I really wanted to write about why teenage girls fawn all over this so-called romance, but really end up hating anything that comes close to it. Half of those girls end up running away with Roxanne in my version of the tale.

Rant #2

"A writer can write anywhere." Yah, that statement is true if you are talking about free-lance writing. I can sure as hell write anywhere when I see something that inspires me. I can pull out a pen and paper in the bathroom of Ruby Tuesday's if I have to and spit out a page or two. It's when I am forced to write about a subject that I have no interest in that I can't write just "anywhere." Hell, I can't even write at all, why? BECAUSE I HAVE NO INTEREST IN IT.

I feel purely insulted that just because I am given an assignment I don't want to write about, I might be considered as not a writer. Not a good writer at least. I have always thought of myself as a writer, that's what I do, and I like to do it too. Just as long as I am writing something I WANT TO WRITE. That's why I have such a problem in school, I think. All this forced writing. It's not healthy. I think we should always get to choose our subject. Everyone would be so into it then, everyone would WANT to write. If it was a research paper they would WANT to research it. And they could probably write about it anywhere, too.

She Was There

She was there. Like every previous, chilly morning she was there. A tall, striking blonde who walked with a false purpose. And his friends all stared. 10:00 A.M. on the short trip from third to fourth period. They gawked and joked, and shared fictionist stories of their own personal experiences with the golden endeavor.

But it didn't matter to him, because *she* was there. In the shadows she remained unseen, except for his eyes to lie upon. Behind the blonde, she also moved with her head up, but the confidence in her eyes was of a different type. And while the blonde walked with grace and style, she alone walked with vitality. She was dressed in baggy green pants and a black sweater, as if to conceal something. Her dyed red hair showed blonde roots, as if she was trying to hide a beauty that was so prominent it screamed to him. Her name was Layla.

Only he had noticed when she arrived in the middle of the year. Strange feelings fixed upon him when he looked in her eyes that seemed to be swimming with colors; grey and blue and green and yellow. Sort of like a feline, but more human than that.

Saturday Night

It was a Saturday night and I was home because of the snow and because my parents are real weird about me driving in less-than-perfect weather. Maybe it was because Heather and I had gotten into a real bad accident about a year ago. No one was really hurt in it, but it scared the bejeezus out of everyone, especially my mom and Heather, who are both Tauruses, but that has nothing to do with this anyway, just a little weird, ya know? Or maybe it was because this one time I backed up right in front of my parents and knocked the mailbox over — but, hey, I had just gotten my license and I was late for work, so, the way I see it, at least I haven't hit a car yet, well, not technically, but I'll tell you about that some other time.

So it was pitch black but still glowing from the snow that seems alive when it first falls. No one has driven in it, so everything is covered with this blanket and, while it's 23 degrees outside, everything looks warm and cozy because it's covered with this one universal wrap of white. I didn't really mind, though, that it was Saturday and I wasn't out. I stayed home and read this book that Mike had told me about. I liked the book a lot but I think I read it mainly because it made me feel like he was near me rather than ten million miles away, so to speak. He was really in Austria, which wasn't technically but might as well have been ten million miles away because it was across the ocean and all. It was really horrible when he left, and I think I cried for ten days, but I'd die before I'd let anyone know that, especially him. It's weird with this guy, ya know, like I can't decide what my deal is or what "our" deal is or if we even *have* a deal. I guess it doesn't matter because even if we did he lives across the ocean, so to speak.

So I was reading and I decided I wanted my mom to curl my hair like she did when I was younger and I had this really long hair that went past my torso. So I heated up these old curlers and she put them in but it wasn't the same. One, because my hair only came down right to my shoulders now, and two, I guess because I was seventeen and the thrill of your mother curling your hair is gone, even though you want it to be there. After we took the curlers out, my hair was real bouncy and Shirley Temple–like, and it reminded me of how I used to want to be Shirley Temple when I took dance classes for nine years, only to drop out because I thought I was too fat to be famous. Truthfully, I think I was too fat, but now I'm just a little overweight but nothing major or horrendous or anything. So my hair was looking cute, but five-year-old cute, and I think it made my face look really pretty, which is really hard for me to admit sometimes because I don't think my face is at all pretty, not like my sister. Anyhow, I stood there looking all innocent and my mother said I was cute and I wondered if she had any idea just how innocent I wasn't. But sometimes I got mad at the fact I wasn't impure enough.

Anyhow, the point was that I sat there on that Saturday night not caring that I wasn't wasting my youth away like everyone else, reading a book that only reminded me that he wasn't here and having this curly hair that reflected a personality that wasn't mine. But I guess it's great that I looked pretty — even though I was home on a Saturday and no one would notice anyway. Plus, I probably didn't even really look pretty, I just thought I did because I was alone with no one there to see it and the moon was all big and the snow made everything beautiful in the way that only nature can. But maybe someone would stop by. Fat chance, though, because of it snowing and the serene calm of the outside sealed my fate on that odd Saturday. I would sit pretty by myself reading, and missing him, and looking innocent for no one but my mother and God, who both probably knew better than to believe this face just because I had blonde angelic curls and was staring out the window at a world that was glowing, making me look insignificant.

Time Story

In heaven the souls of unborn children wait to be given life with heavy anticipation. Bodiless life that longs for a form to mold in and belong to. Every three minuets, thousands of them are given the right to life. Those thousands of souls will transport in and out of bodies until their death. Every time their souls possess a new body, their memories from past lives are erased, but the vacant space will remain seared in their minds forever. Only when they learn to fill that space with substance, an emotion such as love or joy or bliss, can they be ready to return to heaven.

Alice walks home from school and she can't help shake the feeling that this day, Thursday, was her first day of school, in this school, as Alice Bundren. She had walked down the halls that seem to snake around her with lights that charmed her deep green eyes. Hollow faces that never met with her gaze, but called her name and hugged her body, and left her with no feeling at all. Teachers called for assignments, and she reached blindly in her bag and pulled out work, done in her handwriting, but she had no recollection of doing it at all. So she phantomed her day and only looked forward to arriving home.

Home. A house stood before her like a cloud with blue trimmed shutters. Passing through the door the smell of fresh paint hit her. Walking down the hall of her own house she can't seem to find the door to her room, though she knows she must have entered it a thousand mindless times. Only the sign with purple sparkly letters that reads "Alice" tips her off that her room must be inside, just beyond this gate. Tripping over a pair of muddy shoes, she stumbles into the bedroom and her blonde hair catches her eye in the mirror as she walks by it. She studies her reflection as is for the first time, and only her deep emerald eyes seem familiar. She can't help but feel that the face in the mirror is unrecognizable. "But that's impossible," she thinks out loud. This is the same body; I am the same person I have always been. But the olive complexion and vibrant blonde hair betray the feeling, and she can't help but picture herself as a million other people.

The eyes, her eyes, only stare back and seem to mock her sanity.

The Muerte

Before man began to inhabit the plains, two tribes of wild horses ran unfettered in an abundance of luxury. Not even the Indians had begun to take away from their resources. Grass lay in thick green blankets beneath their feet for eating, and crystal pools of water flowed from the north throughout the land for the occasional midday drink. Only one stretch of dust lay in the middle, a divider of the two tribes. It looked like a scar upon the land, the only thing dead, dry, and unmoving among a rhythm of life on either side. The tribes called it Muerte.

To the left of the Muerte, the Cazorp tribe flourished; to the right the Romuhs. The Cazorps were dark and spotted. Their eyes filled with a depth unattained by any creature before. Their leader was Azazel, who was said to have descended from the god of fire. Little colts spread rumors that out of the great blaze that created Muerte, Azazel had been born and left as an offering for taking away their land. No one had ever been able to prove this for Azazel himself was an old stallion, and no other horse matched his age — except for one. Amourha, the leader of the Romuhs, was said to be as old as Azazel, and that only he knew the truth about their origin. He, like the rest of the Romuhs, was light and had a mane of white silk. His eyes were cool blue, and matched the crystal in the water.

It was known across the plains, that the Romuhs stayed to the right of Muerte, and the

Cazorps stayed to the left. Any horse that dared venture across it was left to the fate the opposing tribe put upon it.

It was because of this belief that the Romuhs stood staring with their cerulean eyes at Amourha. "But how can you dare cross the Muerte?!" they began to cry. Amourha's stubborn disposition permeated throughout the huddled tribe. His eyes, though the color of ice, were warm yet firm with his words. "I must go warn Azazel and the Cazorps," he began, "The gods of prophecy have visited me in my sleep. A great monster that walks on his hind legs and has no hair except for the peak of his head is going to invade our land."

The tribe stood motionless in disbelief. Invade? The word held no meaning for them, for the threat was never before presented in their harmonious existence.

"But you can't go . . . what will we do if you don't come back?"

Amourha blinked slowly as if to hold back something, "If I do not return, a new leader will arise from somewhere else of this earth."

With that he turned and began to run towards the Muerte with all the power his four strong muscular legs could force.

By the time he got there, Azazel was already waiting for him. They stared, black eyes against blue, and talked without speaking.

Brother, our time has come.

Azazel reared. *No Amourha, I refuse to believe it.*

Amourha stood steady, without movement. *The gods have visited you too, haven't they? You know what is to happen.*

Azazel's black eyes burned with resistance. *I don't believe in gods, and magic, and prophecy. I am going to stay here, and rule my tribe. If you dare cross the Muerte, I will kill you myself.*

Amourha licked the top of his mouth. *Azazel, you know I must cross.*

Azazel bared his teeth. *So be it.*

As if in slow motion, the two horses galloped across the land that had never before been tread upon. Straight to each other, they met in the middle and began to fight. In slow motion, the yellow dust whirled as the stallions danced around one another with a sort of demonic grace. Each taking another blow, they fought with vigor, one for his own life, one for the future of his kind. Both tribes had by this time come and stood on either side watching their leader, their god, rumble his only parallel force.

So enthralled with the savage display in front of them, no one had begun to notice the sky's resentment as it boiled into dark clouds of thunder and lighting. As Amourha and Azazel both lunged for each other for the last time, the sky sent down a powerful bolt that surged through both the bodies and then into the dust. The brothers fell, one on top of the other, in a silent defeat. The tribes stared at one another in disbelief, vulnerable. Slowly they walked towards the death that lay in front of them, and began to place blame.

"Your leader has killed Amourha! You all must die!" was heard over " Azazel will be avenged!" A great battle unfolded just as man began to walk up the river.

Too busy fighting to notice, horses from both tribes began to fall by the prick of man's arrow. Some were harnessed and forced into slavery. Some died slowly and bled away into the Muerte. The few that escaped remain today, fearfully roaming the plains. If you catch yourself in the view of one, be careful. Their eyes, whether blue or black, will look at you with such sadness for the life they so carelessly gave away, and they will haunt you forever.

Diary of Someone in 1962

August 31, 1962

Dear Diary,

So today is my 25th birthday and all around me people are reminiscing, or telling me that I'm still too young to know better, or reminding me that I am closer to 30 than ever now and it is time to start acting like a grown up. I think to myself, "I am a grown up." I just never grew out of my adolescent habits. And why should that be a bad thing, I ask you?

I've never been much for birthdays — all I can think of is two plus five is seven and that is how old I was when I learned to ride a bike. When I was younger we lived on a very steep hill and it was impossible for an adult to ride up and down it, let alone a five-year-old girl. So when we moved here to Rockville it was much easier on the flat ground and Daddy drove me to a yard sale and let me pick out whatever bike my heart desired. I picked the purple one; I've always been fond of purple.

Besides, I think the best presents are the ones that are presents for no special occasion. Oh, don't feel too sad, I still very much appreciate you, dear diary, as a birthday present today from Jane. She's always been a thoughtful sister, harsh with her tongue but at least gentle with her actions. How sneaky she is, always acting oblivious to my interests and dislikes and then gets me a diary the day after I finish the last page of my old one. In any event, I still like presents that take you by surprise, that come out of nowhere — that way you know the person really wanted to buy you something. Usually people only buy things when they have to. But Daddy bought me a bike for no reason. That day was 72 degrees and beautiful — I could have ridden that bike all the way back home.

December 1

Dear Diary,

As I approach the end of this year I have started to think about its events. I have come to realize that I have no lover, no father, no advancement in my job, and an incredible indifference to my family and their lives. Sometimes I want to join Daddy, I don't care if it's in heaven, limbo, or hell. I'll go right to St. Peter and demand to know where he is, then I'll go there and just sit and talk and feel the comfort that used to consume me when I was little and I'd fall asleep in his lap. I think that was the only time I really felt safe my entire life. Mother and I were cleaning out Daddy's desk and I found in the bottom drawer, way in the back, rocks. Now diary you must understand, when I was a little girl we would go to Carlsbad every summer for a month and on the beach would be these incredibly smooth, profound rocks. I thought rocks were really something then. I would fill my sand bucket with them and then lug them all the way back home, making my luggage about fifteen pounds heavier. Then I would paint them and give them as presents to Mother and Daddy and Jane and Kevin and Jay. Now, of course, my brothers used them as ammunition in their war games, and my sister threw them out with her dolls, and Mother never liked anything "junky," as she called it lying around the house. But here, twenty years later, here are the rocks that I painted right here in Daddy's bottom drawer, tucked away like a fond memory in the back of your mind. Oh, dear Father, why did it have to be you that went, the lord could have taken me instead. You gave so much to this family, community, country, world, and universe; here I remain, small and pathetic with nothing to offer but a puppy named Sam and this old journal.

December 11

Diary,

So it's been four days since I decided to stop going to work. I can just imagine the faces of those men when sweet little April is not there to write their words for them, to put together their precious presentations, to pour their coffee. I wonder, gentlemen, whose rear end will you now stare at when you drop your file? Certainly not mine, not ever again. Mother asked me to come for Kevin's birthday, but I thought to myself, "Self, why should you go when Kevin hasn't bothered to even call you since last July when he needed that four hundred dollars?" So I decided that Sam and I would have a quality evening together reading Faulkner. Sam especially likes the little dog in "The Bear" — he yelps happily when I read it out loud. This wretched little cat stares at Sam through the window some nights and drives him absolutely insane. Mrs. Henvomorra the landlady told me I'd be evicted "if that dog doesn't shut his trap." Horrible old woman, she's only jealous because not even a dog will love her. She'll be bitter for the rest of her life. But not me, diary! I have you and Faulkner and little old Sam here, so why should I worry? I can live off the money Daddy left for me for about six months, and I think that is all the time I have left in this world anyway. Who needs to live to be twenty-six?

December 25

Diary,

I fear this will be my last entry because I have grown tired of you. Today is Christmas so I thought I'd give you one last visit before I put you back onto the bookshelf for good. I think Faulkner, Goethe, Rilke, and good old Louisa May will be good company for you. I thought of calling Mother and the others, but the thought of talking to all of them and explaining why I haven't returned their phone calls and letters would be too draining and besides, I didn't care how they were or if they were upset that I had cut myself off from them. We are all going to die someday, what difference does it make if you live like you're dead? The same consequences will be put into effect I just thought I'd save them the time. I think I'm not going to try and visit Daddy anymore, because I believe Daddy is impossible to visit. I know diary, you think I'm crazy, but hear me out. The day Daddy died and we put his graying flesh into the earth and piled the dirt on top of him, he ceased to exist. Even St. Peter was a lie that old Mother told me to both frighten and console me when I was little. Everything you are told when you are little is a lie. So now diary, Merry Christmas, I think Sam and I will follow Father into that realm of nothingness soon, life is too exhausting for me, and the weather rather cold.

Conclusion

And though I'd like to stay
I know it is now my time to leave
But before I go
I take a minute to look around and breathe
These words and images
They are all a part of me
This girl that I got to know is nowhere to be seen
Also, I look and widely open up my eyes
There is a mirror standing directly in front of me
My eyes penetrate my reflection
And my fears begin to melt
I am a better person
When I take the time
To look inside myself